THE CASTLE

AND THE BETRAYAL OF NATHAN GLASS

JM HENDRIKX

PROLOGUE: RAFFAELLO RIVIERA

The Riviera Family was composed of tall women who lounged languidly in taffeta gowns with pinched noses and haughty smiles; and of short men in Cuban heeled boots, with creases between their serious eyes and spinach between their vicious little teeth. The Rivieras had the most elegant stolen furniture and the most mouth-watering jewels in every colour and hue. They were amazingly unpopular and extremely unconcerned, for they had magic and magic was everything.

The Riviera family produced stronger magicians with every generation born. So, the pattern of proud yet jealous parents became a familiar ailment that allowed for much wailing and dramatic hand gesturing within the walls of Stonerock castle. The last of the Rivieras, the runt of the short males, was Raffaello Riviera. He was born with clenched fists and a look of indignation that never really left him and was distinctly present the day he burned out. For with great magicians their finest hour is always their last. They burn out with intention, give up their life and all of their power in one final explosion of glory.

Raffaello was a furious colicky baby, a biting, scratching, face-kicker of a toddler and a precocious, bulbous-faced teenager. No-one loved him, not even his mother, Cecelia Riviera, who was tall and poised and referred to him in the past tense, as if he was no longer in existence. His father found him irksome and told him so, exactly three days before he, Constantine Riviera, died from choking on an oversized horse chestnut.

The day after that, Raffaello sat between his maiden aunts on a beautiful Louis XV sofa feeling like a wombat between two giraffes. He was utterly miserable: engulfed in grief and the strong scent from their over-applied face powder. The high pitch of their tinkling laughter above his head and the clinking of fine bone china close to his ears, made him want to sink through the floorboards and disappear forever. They asked him to magic more sugar for their tea. He stood up and stomped out of the tea room in childish rebellion, but they did not notice. He walked all the way to Escaville to find them their sugar, as his heart was so heavy that he could not muster a simple spell.

Raffaello rarely went to Escaville and he always felt panicky and confused when he did, which was how he ended up in the blacksmith's asking for sugar and with the owner laughing at him. He thought he would explode with fury, being laughed at by Angus Savine, a grimy faced, non-castle living man. Instead he burst into tears, his watery, dark brown eyes streaming like a broken pipe.

Angus gave him a hug and then lifted him up with strong arms to sit upon his workbench. The squat young man convulsed with sadness. Angus made him a jam sandwich and gave him a glass of milk. Such kindness was sweet and soothing to Raffaello's soul; yet not as sweet as the apricot jam which made the surface of his tongue dance. He ate it anyway. Kindness had always tasted strange. This was the day that he met Claudia the blacksmith's daughter. She sauntered in cheerfully; intrigued by his presence she said hello, jumped up to sit next to him and smiled a wonderful, welcoming smile. He felt a zinging sensation of warmth rushing through him. He tried to return the smile, but looked as if he had just been asked to show her his teeth. She grinned widely, reached across for his sandwich and took a bite. He felt as if he was slowly dissolving into her golden glow.

Claudia Savine had playful instincts, tousled hair and could skim stones better than anyone else in the world. His first and only friend; she made him laugh and he stopped being angry, she made him feel comfortable and he stopped showing off. Claudia was real magic too, extremely gifted, yet not as skilled as he.

Before Claudia, Raffaello had used his magic mostly to fulfil the boring and complicated requests of his parents or for serious experimentation during the long hours he spent being ignored in the castle. Claudia only knew how to play.

One day they sat on a bench overlooking the canal as Eleanor Raye, the town parfumier walked past in a waft of pine, nutmeg and vanilla. She had black hair plaited down her back and a knitted beret upon her head. Within a blink of an eye the hat was a grey cat, curled up contentedly and purring. Raffaello's mouth dropped open and Claudia grinned. She looked back. Eleanor had not noticed the change, but Claudia saw that Eleanor's hair was different. Black ants had taken its place and now meandered furiously in the perfect cascade of her plait. Eleanor scratched her neck and the cat leapt from her head. By the time it landed it was just a knitted beret and her glossy dark locks had returned. Raffaello grabbed Claudia in an embrace, so that Eleanor would not catch their eye as she looked around in bewilderment. They held their breath and held back their laughter, whilst looking into each other's eyes. When it was safe to look away, when Eleanor had gone, they paused, smiling and then kissed.

Days of idle magic continued. They created waterfalls that thundered and roared to the beat of their favourite songs as they splashed and danced in the shallows. They concocted pink translucent lizards with candyfloss hair, exploding cantaloupes and a gazelle carousel; as well as trouble for those near them when they were in high spirits. Raffaello particularly enjoyed elevating the barber's shop from the ground. The owner's eyebrows would jump to his hairline and his mouth would open tunnel-wide as he cursed loudly in his native tongue. They would wait and watch him tell the story of what had happened, with his expressive face and large hands, to every customer who came in. Raffaello and Claudia laughed until it hurt with every disbelieving head shake and pat on the back that he received.

Claudia Savine knew she was beautiful. She knew that Essie Fossie's boys had no need for two dozen horse shoes and that Alex Bryanny did not require yet another garden fork for his mother. And so did her father whose kind welcome disappeared when the eager boys came into his blacksmith's shop. He would send Claudia out the back so that he could serve them; his firm hand closed the door behind her with a resounding bang. Through the crack she would watch their faces fall and revel in their disappointment, her eyes sparkling with mischief.

Raffaello made songbirds appear at Claudia's window in the morning and different flowers grow around her dressing table mirror each day. Their fragrance would lift her spirits and she would smile and think of him. A necklace of the most intricate and unusual design would appear around her neck each time she thought him; so she thought of him frequently.

Claudia loved the way handsome men would look so perplexed when they saw her with Raffaello. They would often stop and stare mid sentence, mid mouthful and midway between a safe place and a lamppost. It was such fun. Raffaello would hold her hand tightly, his brown eyes alive with happiness.

Summer came and she decided to try out love. A game of let's pretend. So that she would know how to do it properly when it was the real thing, and because she knew Raffaello would love her back with all of his heart. One warm evening, without permission, she took her father's boat; whilst Raffaello stole the most cherished of his mother's champagne from the castle cellar. Together they sailed into the night, danced on the deck, shucked oysters, toasted their parents' health, delighted in their misbehaviour, drank the bottles dry and fell asleep under the stars.

When they returned two days later Raffaello felt as free as the silver eagles that flew over Stonerock castle. As a child he had watched them and hated them because they were powerful and beautiful, but now he felt as if he were one of them. He walked home from Escaville, his arms outstretched, the muscles of his face relaxed as his heart soared above him.

Then summer was gone; its warmth and sweet scent had faded silently away. And so too was Claudia Savine who had become decidedly unavailable; and so too was Raffaello's heart. He became distraught, believing that her absence meant his end. Angus Savine said Claudia was at Cavanagans with friends or shopping with her mother or not feeling well again. Angus would hammer the metal with a new found ferocity the more desperate Raffaello became, and Raffaello became more and more desperate. Angus saw the wildness in Raffaello's mind; saw it clearly in every expression, every movement. Angus was unnerved, reminded of the brutal face of Constantine Riviera. In the calmer moments of his distress Raffaello sat very upright and his sadness transformed into disdain and scorn: the face of his mother, Cecelia Riviera. Raffaello would sit on the pavement outside the shop, listening to the clang of metal on metal and wait for hours, but he would always miss her.

Once he saw her in the market, with a boy he did not know, under the stone archway, wearing a necklace he did not recognise, but before he could get to her she vanished into the crowd. She had seen him and he knew she had, but she did not wait.

The truth was so dark and scary that he could not bear to look at it. One Saturday morning, when Angus told him Claudia was too busy to see him, he put his face uncomfortably close to Angus's and with hot breath shouted, 'Liar!' Their eyes connected in aggression and then in fear because both men knew that something inside Raffaello had just snapped. Silently they stared, for a brief and intense moment, before the world resumed its ways and the anvil struck and the door slammed.

Raffaello's heart seethed with blackness, his temples pounded with rage and he ran; through the town, through the forest, gasping in short sharp breaths. His heart beat like a military drum growing louder; it resonated through his whole body. He reached home, his chest painfully tight. He crashed through the corridors of the castle and flung open heavy cupboard doors searching for his crossbow. When he found it, he grabbed it and charged up the staircase of the East Tower. He ran to the very top breathless as he stood outside in the cool air. Sweat ran down his face, the salt taste now in his mouth, he took aim. One by one he shot down the silver eagles of the southern forest and their death cries found no mercy in his heart.

So distraught was Raffaello when he entered the great hall, so uncoordinated in his steps, so dishevelled in his attire that his mother looked up from her game of bridge in the far corner of the room and noticed him. As disapproval filled her eyes he took up his crossbow once more: so that he would never again have to feel her ice. His mother's friends put on their gloves, clicked their bags tightly closed and silently fumed that they would need to find a new bridge partner by next Wednesday week.

And so Raffaello, only child, last of the Rivieras, was alone in the castle with furniture to marvel at, gems that dazzled and a heart that felt as if it were bleeding on to the floor. He paced the corridors, his mouth paper dry, his body shaking. Perhaps it was his mother's stare or the turbulence in the cauldron of his heart that defined what he, as the greatest living magician of his time, did next. He thought of every grievance, minor or major, that had occurred throughout his life: from the baker who had once sold him stale bread, to the circus bears who had scared him as a child, to Claudia Savine and all of her family. Even the elder Savines, the best code breakers in the land, who could shatter or dismantle the most impenetrable of curses and enchantments, would not be able to stop his magic. He knew he was strong enough.

His revenge was to be a storm. He would banish from the island and place in perpetual winter all those who had ever wronged him. He refined his magic, smiling softly, as he paced the corridors of the castle; an adult version of the precocious child he once was. He wrung his hands as his mind twisted and turned. His whispers muffled and indecipherable travelled the castle like freed ghosts. His passion with all its fire and intensity would go into his last ever spell, from which he wanted to burn out and end his pain.

At dusk he returned to the top of the East Tower, where the winds raced. He breathed in the sea air, focused on the darkening sky. Slowly the unlucky ones appeared; blown in from all directions. Forced through the air, some fought, some surrendered, but all were gathered up and delivered into the spiralling tumult of the storm as it raged above the sea. He was about to place Claudia in the centre. Her brightness clouded over, her hair lashed her face, all colour drained from her as she watched the people below her. Then she looked at him. He saw her fear and he loved her and for a second he weakened. That second caused the flaw.

To quell the light, blackness rose in his heart. There was a blinding flash as he turned their eyes an icy topaz blue, so that they would always be marked. Marked as the accursed people of the Winter Storm. With its work done the storm raced out to sea, where it would only rest in the deepest most hostile winters. In places where the cold cut into your bones, the sun existed mostly as memory and every part of your being ached with despair and regret. A storm that would move them on to new territory should the harshness of the environment ever abate.

Hawks circled Stonerock castle now that the eagles were gone. They looked down where Raffaello lay collapsed. He heard the crash of the waves, felt the cold stone floor against his face, the weight of his damp clothes, the taste of the sea. He did not open his eyes. He knew he had failed to burn out, that it was morning and he was still alive. His lips parted and his body juddered as he cried quietly without tears. He went to shout in anger, but only a feeble voice arose. In frustration he banged his forehead repeatedly on the floor. He knew what remained was a tiny ember; a memory of a warm day on the deck of a boat, hands entwined, feet in the water and time seeming to stand still. Love. Crack. He split open his skull. The pain's intensity was needed to start the fire, to remedy the flaw, to ensure they never returned. He needed to end it all, to burn out.

The dragon of his wrath grew before him; it became real,

living, breathing, muscular and strong. Its breath warmed the floor on which he lay. This was the Firebrand, his creation, his legacy, his dragon; programmed to destroy the people of the Winter Storm, should they ever set foot on these shores again. The dragon's eyes held a determination grown from sorrow and its veins pulsed with the rage that had so tormented Raffaello.

The dragon roared and Raffaello felt heat on his face, steam rising. He opened his eyes. In his last moments he saw the Firebrand, alight in its magnificence, skin glowing hot like a blacksmith's iron, as the burning stone seared his tearless cheek.

PART I

50 years after the burn out of Raffaello Riviera

STONEROCK CASTLE AND THE MAGIC FOUR

*A*nnabelle Drake started many things that she did not finish. Her thoughts bounced around just as she did. Good ideas were as fleeting as fireworks. She never finished writing the history of Stonerock Castle, in which she lived, although it had once seemed like a good idea.

The stories we tell to other people and to ourselves are flawed; each history has many versions. So, when digging up the past, we may find buried treasure or excavate something more alarming. Something hard to remove, that is even harder to put back and that may catch and snare on its way out. Annie's initial enthusiasm was like a spade that sent the soil flying. She did not realise that the ground beneath was just about to reveal something dangerous. Annie had become bored, so she dropped the spade and walked off. She never read the final version; she never knew. They tried to protect her.

For centuries magic existed on the island like a gentle breeze. Then, as if the breeze wanted a voice, it became a whoosh, which swept through the island as people realised their extraordinary talents. It grew louder with each year that passed. Eventually the voice of magic broke, like ocean waves, with the burn out of Raffaello Riviera.

The servants of Stonerock inherited the castle upon his death, with the instruction to enjoy it fully. They played canaster and drank everything in the cellar. Liveryman Griswald Goat, who wore no shoes, was king of the card games and entertainment. He would sit at the end of the table laughing loudly and barking orders. Cards would fly like humming birds' wings in amazing shuffling displays. Between games they would perform short plays or dances, which they made up on the spot.

The most exceptional magician of his or her generation is known as the Scion. The Scion rises with power that clearly surpasses everything that has come before. He or she is considered to be a descendent of magic itself (and not necessarily a descendent of the former greatest magician). It is believed that powerful forces in the universe fire forward, converge and culminate to produce something of stronger concentration each time a Scion is born. The Scion is revered until the rising Scion, the next greatest one, arrives.

The magical eminence of the Riviera family ended with the death of Raffaello. His remaining relatives were incomparable; they were swindlers, toadies, peddlers, meddlers, and one accordion player. The servants gossiped about the next Scion and concluded that it would come from one of two magic families: the Drakes or the Cavangans.

Griswald was godfather to Horatio Drake and as a betting man, Griswald's money was firmly wagered on the boy. Griswald, like many others, believed that Stonerock castle was meant to be the seat of power for the greatest magician.

One by one the servants passed away. The last one left was Griswald Goat. The castle had run to ruin. In his old age he lived mostly in the pantry and the courtyard where he would sunbathe and watch the clouds. When the old Goat died, my father Horatio Drake inherited the castle. He married the beautiful Esther Valencia; she took his surname, as his magic lineage was stronger. They were soo in love and lived happily in Stonerock Castle. They had three children: obstinate Aldemus, bossy Louisa and the marvellous Annabelle Drake.

My father is one of the Magic Four, two male and two female magicians born in the same year, whose skills are exceptional.

Separated from their peers by their extraordinary experiences, magic brought them close together. Destiny and magic intertwined as the Magic Four married each other. The stronger magic line, decided by the marrying couple, determined their surnames. So Frederick Hayler married Violet Cavanagan and graciously took her surname. My mother's birth name of Valencia was swallowed up by the powerful Drake pedigree! A discussion in which they were either unanimously unified or that simmered for eight days like a fuming, spitting oil pan depending on whom you ask.

Together Esther and Horatio Drake transformed the castle into the meeting place for magic minds, a house of lively debate, laughter and the most outrageous magic experiments. A perfect place for the Scion to rise and it could be one of them!

THE FIRST LETTER

HORATIO JACK ALGERNON DRAKE ESQUIRE
STONEROCK CASTLE

Dear Annie

It pleases me greatly, that you are writing the history of our home. Such a wonderful idea! In answer to your questions, for inclusion in your book, I hope this helps:

My lasting and treasured memories of my godfather are of him in the cellar wearing a paper crown as he played cards. Even numbers of players were better for card games. A blush-pink chaise longue with clawed feet had been taken from Cecelia Riviera's former dressing room and placed at the end of the card table. It was known as 'the odd one out chair' because the one who was slowest to the table for cards had to sit out the first three games on it. And boy did they run to get there. The chef was a gigantic man, but I never remember him reclining on it. I do remember him wheezing loudly and sprinting faster than I thought possible along the corridors to get to the table when the clock chimed 7.00pm.

I also remember seeing the pot-scrubber and the pianist being tied to various large objects or the banisters just before 7.00pm and them struggling frantically to escape. Griswald was always calmly waiting to begin.

Griswald was scrawny, yet fit as a fiddle from a life spent riding and tending to horses. He ate anchovies and peanuts for breakfast most mornings. I remember the heady smell of fish and salt. He told me he was raised on a diet of chips and egg, with the occasional addition of ketchup, when funds would allow. The latter part of his life, (which he referred to as his cheese toastie years, and that was all I ever ate when I visited him!), were by far his happiest years.

The formation of the Magic Four marked our coming of age; the beginning of a new era. I am so proud to have learned from and worked with all of them. If you are going to list experiments and achievements please include the Stone-carved poetry spell, Violet's Waiting Room, Fred's work with black hearts, and Esther's Flourishes.

You, Aldemus and Louisa are the history to come and I am incredibly excited for all of you.

Daddy

x

THE SECOND LETTER

CAVANAGANS
NORTHERN FOREST
NR ESCAVILLE

Dear Annie

A history. Yes, you are the best one to write it. I will now get a skeleton out of the closet and show it to you. Your father has agreed that it is time. So, this is my version of our history, with a change that should be included. I hope this helps. I love what you have written so far. You need to know that in the beginning there were not four of us, but five.

Some people are born to be together. As a five we were meant to be friends, it worked so perfectly and we all knew it. There was an atmosphere of hope that grew stronger the more we discovered what we could do. We were like a family, in the most imperfect sense. A well meaning criticism from Horatio to Frederick would send Frederick into a wild fury, because he would know Horatio was right and would be angry for not seeing it first. Wonderful arguments and strong emotions would bubble and sizzle, as we were all passionate about using magic for the greater good.

As we grew older there seemed to be a natural order of who would end up marrying who, which sounds strange, but seemed quite clear to all of us, I think. Horatio was supremely confident and headstrong, and the only one who could take him down a peg or two with any success, was Esther (and how we would cheer when she did!). She was also the prettiest and he loved beautiful things. Frederick was the reserved one, a deep thinker and well I don't have to tell you about me... it was all about balancing, now I look back at it.

And that left one. Nathan. In some ways he was the most perfect of us. I think his weaknesses were not as weak as ours and his strengths were just as strong. Perhaps he was the Scion. He felt very alone. We tried to keep him included. When your brother Aldemus was born your father asked Nathan to be his godfather and Nathan went off the rails.

He completely withdrew. He left his house, never returned and lived in the southern forest where he was working with lightning bolts and trying to control the weather. Every day one of us would go into the forest to talk to him, but he would not speak to anyone. He never slept, just worked constantly on his experiments. He found the tallest tree, attached steel rods to it and tried to conduct lightning and channel its energy. One day during a storm he caught the lightening. Horatio and Esther saw a huge flash in the forest and ran out in the rain to see if he was safe. They found the burnt out tree. In the sky was a huge cloud of glittering black smoke.

As you know, real magic people rarely die of old age; instead they burn out. The strongest magic is created this way. When Esther and Horatio saw the tree and the cloud and no Nathan, they knew that was what he had done. The storm left and the black clouds travelled out with it. The darkness was created. It is strong and powerful, because Nathan was. None of us have really been able to come to terms with what happened, with what he created, so we don't talk about him very often.

He was great man. I feel sad writing this. When the clouds come I think of the rain as his tears and the thunder as his rage.

Violet Cavanagan

THE THIRD LETTER

Dear Annie

Violet has covered what's important, but as I'm the 'deep thinker' I thought I should contribute.

I've been searching the depths of my memory, adopting serious and contemplative poses, as I sit in my chair.

I've discovered, much to my disappointment, that my memory is remarkably shallow. Vast swathes of my past seem to have evaporated. So, these are the only cheap gems I have for you:

- Griswald Goat reminded me of a scarecrow, such a weather beaten look about him.

- The Cavanagan name has a great lineage, but getting the girl was all that mattered to me!

Love Annie, that's what life is all about. Everything else is on the sidelines.

All the best

Frederick Cavanagan

Ps) I'm looking forward to reading your history to find out what happened!

THE FINAL LETTER

Dear Annabelle

I have read your history tonight. I would like to add this:

Nathan retreated to the forest and focused on his magic, because it was all he had left. He faked his own burn out. He felt his own heart going black. He is truly mad now, but has brief flashes of sanity and moments when he remembers how it was when he wasn't like this. Like this moment right now.

I am in your room. I had come to kill you, but I saw you sleeping and you looked so much like Esther when she was young. So I sat at your writing desk, read your history and the letters. I wrote this instead.

I saw Esther's paintings on your wall. Their likeness to your father as a young man is striking. Look at your father's eyes in the one by the cedar trees, with his arms around her. What do those eyes tell you?

Now I know for sure.

There must be some part of my heart that is not black and is shining as I write, but that will soon be gone. I will come back and destroy you all.

Nathan

VIOLET CAVANAGAN'S WAITING ROOM

Twenty-five years before Annabelle Drake wrote the History of Stonerock Castle

*H*oratio Drake went with Violet Cavanagan into her newly created Waiting Room and she took him through with delight. The room was carpeted in soft grey with black chairs upholstered in charcoal and cream stripes. They sat for a short time, Horatio very upright and alert, Violet hardly able to conceal her excitement. On the wall in front of them appeared an open doorway into the night sky. He looked at the doorway and grinned at her. Then they both ran forward and jumped out with freedom and recklessness, as if they were children jumping into the sea. As their bodies plummeted they circled, duck dived and somersaulted, hair wild about their faces, then they landed gracefully on the pavement below at the same time.

He looked around, taking everything in. She took him to the car she had acquired and parked. It was midnight blue and luxurious. It was not exactly hers, but she was planning on returning it with the dent removed, a full tank of petrol and of course any damage that Horatio would no doubt do repaired, for she knew that he would not for one moment sit in the passenger seat.

They got in the car. He examined everything in front of him.

'This is good. I believe you now,' he said.

He beamed at her and felt almost proud. She rolled her eyes.

'Ah, you believe me now, you sceptic.'

'I thought you'd inflicted one of your dreams on me. That this was some kind of trick. Now I'm impressed.'

'Perhaps this Waiting Room, this entrance to another world, is the work of the greatest magician; Violet Cavanagan the rising Scion,' she said and grinned, looking forward to his reaction.

Horatio put the key in the ignition.

'Perhaps,' he replied with a matching smile, refusing to be provoked, then accelerated with such force and screech that any further taunting was quickly flung from Violet's mind.

THERE WAS A BOOKSHOP IN SOHO. It smelled of fresh coffee and old books. The ceilings were high and windows vast for a small, tucked away shop. Horatio's eyes opened wide, his whole being relaxed. Violet watched her friend fall in love as he looked around and she felt extremely pleased.

'I want it,' he said as he held up a book and placed it across his chest.

'The book?'

'The shop.'

'Thought so. I think it would go beautifully on the third floor in the West Tower.'

'Good light, but the dimensions are wrong. I don't want curved bookshelves.'

'No. We copy this exactly as it is. The inside will just be different to the outside. We've done it with magic in Cavanagans, around the bar area.'

Horatio sighed, crossed his arms and tapped his fingers impatiently on the book.

'Fine. Let's do it.'

And the library, which Violet liked to refer to as her gift to Horatio, satisfied him immensely. For Horatio gobbled up poetry books like a starved child. He had an amazing memory and could recite any poem he had ever read by heart.

For those who did not know Horatio well, his poetic outbursts defined him as being pretentious. They believed that he loved the sound of his own voice and the occasional applause. The last two facts are undoubtedly true, but those close to him knew that Horatio struggled with expressing his feelings. He could not always discern what his feelings were, even when they would overpower him with brute force. Violet and Frederick Cavanagan believed Horatio's bravado, his showmanship, was to compensate for what he could not show and did not know how to show. Poetry did for him what he could not do for himself.

His friends were mostly entertained by his recitals, although not by the melancholy ones, which Horatio expressed far too well. It was always hard to tell what his girlfriend, Esther Valencia, thought. She would drift off, either deep in thought about what he was saying or contemplating something entirely different and hardly listening; no one was ever quite sure.

HORATIO DRAKE'S STONE-CARVED POETRY SPELL

*S*ometimes Horatio woke up and music or a poem would be playing in his mind. He was never sure if the sound woke him as it began or if it had been gently running as a soundtrack to his slumber. If it was music he would often head to the piano and play it in his pyjamas. If it was poetry he would recite it as he went about his morning routine, often with one or two lines repeating as if they were important to him for some reason he was unaware of.

Horatio never wanted to be forgotten. Worse than to die was to be forgotten. For no living memory to contain any trace of him, that was pure terror.

Early one morning as a child, his father took him to see the moon deer in a remote part of the southern forest. The ground was moist; the air fresh from rain and sunlight was breaking through the trees. There they discovered, amidst magnificent rock formations, tall stone columns with intricate carvings. These lines of pattern and script were both foreboding and fascinating to him. For years people had hoped it would be ancient magic. When it was eventually translated it was writing that described nature, the sun setting and rising. As he stood in streaks of sunlight, he knew then, as he placed paper over the text and shaded away with his pencil to make a copy, that the best way to let your magic live forever was to carve it in stone. The thought never left him.

His love for poetry sprang from books that his grandmother had used to prop up wobbly table legs. His heart was gripped vice-like by the sad ones, as he lay awake reading them aloud to his teddy bear, words that stayed with him. He could recall them all, every poem he had read and did so most evenings, whispering them when he should have been asleep. He lay in the dark, the smell of bacon snaking up the stairs, listening to the clink of plates and the rocking of the table below, the books held closed and close to his heart, hugged tightly to his chest.

Horatio created the Stone-carved poetry spell to act a signal, to mark events. A line of perfect poetry, selected from the myriad of collections in his head, would appear ornately carved in stone to act as a starting gun, a fanfare to a significant occasion or point in time. Sometimes too, it acted as a carefully selected accompaniment, often witty and entertaining. It worked to wondrous effect for occasions of solemnity and mirth. It was met with approval or laughter and always appeared artistically, in harmony with its environment. Horatio, who avoided uncertainty and disliked surprises in general, was in love with this spell and its glorious unpredictability. He looked forward to what it would produce with a sense of complete trust, as he was always pleased with the result. Planning the castle events drew Horatio and Esther together. Horatio loved it when they would laugh or gasp at the spell's words. He liked to think that by transference he was as equally impressive, to all who observed him, as the spell.

Living in a stone castle gave the spell plenty of room for

expression, but there were also steps, kitchen floors, picnic rocks and even a town monument that had been gifted by the Stone-carved poetry spell. The Stone-carved floors of his friends in the town of Escaville were regarded either with luminescent pride or heavy shoulders and a desire to buy a rug.

His favourite carving was on a bridge; where he and his son Aldemus had spent a day fishing, which was disrupted by otters and ended with the two of them splashing in the shallows and playing chase. The sun was warm; the water cool, everything seemed right with the world and he knew his devotion to his son was complete and utter. During those flashes of joy that punctured his heart and floored him with his own vulnerability, words appeared like a children's rhyme on the bridge before them. He looked at them and was filled with a deep sense of satisfaction. Aldemus read them, smiling widely, hugging Horatio with arms and legs like a bear cub who knew he was loved.

On days when Esther was being quiet, when Louisa seemed to have completely forgotten who Horatio was, when the castle guests were as dull as his worst fears allowed and neither Annabelle's games nor Aldemus's energy could take the edge off his need for attention, he would wander to the bridge. He would sit on it a while, with his legs dangling over or if the weather was warm might turn up his trousers and walk bare foot through the river. Looking up at the words reminded him that on that day, at that time, in that moment, he was doing a good job of being a father, that he had got it right, that he was ok. It was set in stone.

The summer of the Stone-carved poetry spell coincided with many celebrations. Horatio and Esther loved parties and hosted them often so that they (she) could plan the evening and they (he) could decide the magic performances to be played out. The Stone-carved poetry spell would work its magic throughout the celebrations to suit the mood, rituals and individuals. The spell flicked through the collections in Horatio's mind to select the perfect accompaniments.

Some lines would vanish, while the ones they longed to stay were always held in stone, reminders of wonderful evenings, bad jokes and memorable experiments. If, after time, familiarity bred contempt and the lines became irksome or irrelevant to Horatio the words would leave quietly and politely, without being noticed.

However, the spell extended no such generosity to people outside of the castle. Not for the man who walked twice daily past a garden wall where the spell had carved a sentence designed to alleviate the weight of one's mortality. The unalleviated man, tutted at it, sneered and occasionally mumbled 'graffiti'. Sometimes the words would suddenly increase in size, with a jump intended to startle him, to grab his attention, to make him read them over and let them stay in his head a while, like an unwanted song. The words wriggled around his iron-clad thoughts of disgruntlement and his seething sneer would linger longer.

Horatio's second favourite was in the bathroom; a single line of wicked humour relating to the conversations of an evening with some pompous guests. It was timed to greet Frederick Cavanagan as he entered, escaping their latest long-winded tale. The audacity of the line of poetry reduced Fred to tears of laughter and he struggled to regain composure. Twice he tried to leave with a straight face and waistcoat and twice he fell about laughing before he could open the door properly. When he did, he showed Horatio and they laughed together. Then the words at the end of the poetry departed and a couple of letters shifted, to reveal a different message. A permanent sentence of wisdom profound and true, but to Fred and Horatio the missing words and moved letters were a nod and a wink to the outrageous original sentence, a waspish attack on self-absorption. The new sentence was a line that he and Horatio would repeat to each other when the situation required noble wisdom, with a knowing smile, slight and identified only by each other.

Horatio had a frequently recurring dream. That he was a boy in the forest looking at the towering columns of carved rock for the first time. He would gaze in awe and the word Scion would appear menacingly in front of him, then expand to take over the stone. He would feel afraid, and then he would hear the clinking of plates, the rocking of the table and the smell of bacon from his childhood home. Then he would be wide-awake, unsettled and completely disorientated.

FREDERICK CAVANAGAN'S WORK
WITH BLACK HEARTS

rederick Cavanagan was a scientist and a magician. He found that the knowledge of both intertwined beautifully, that it was easy and joyful to bring them together. Science and magic were like two friends who were always pleased to see each other, that delighted in the eccentricity of the other and encouraged the daredevil spirit. Together they talk for hours, laugh loudly, wear peculiar accessories, such as razor shells, gold measuring spoons or beaded necklaces of live, rolled up centipedes. They might sometimes forget important things such as shoes, but together their more alarming peccadilloes are effortlessly ironed out. Then the gallivanting can begin, with so much more mischief to be had in good company!

Fred's thoughts went like this: I want to do a scientific experiment, but it is particularly risky and dangerous, I value my hands and I am quite used to this face. Never fear my friend, magic is here. It sounds like a wonderful plan. Let's do it. I'll protect you or replicate your face, should we mess things up.

Then, before you know it, bam goes the garden shed in a

riot of indigo flames, all four walls blasted away. Out from the smoking embers staggers a yelping, soot covered Fred. Without trouble and with a beauty that belies the mess before him, the elements of the explosion set to work like a ballet, effortlessly righting, reclaiming and restoring. The burnt smell is overpowering at first, streaked across with chemical edges, but the scent reduces at speed. By the time it vanishes and the cool green fragrances of the woodland have returned, Fred is clean, attired in a new waistcoat; the boards are rearranged and swept up into the trees to form a pleasing tree house from the wreckage, perfectly constructed with black edging. Fred sits in it, scratching his head, magic and science sitting comfortably side by side in his mind, wondering exactly what went wrong, what needs to be done differently next time and if a tree house is actually better than a shed.

So the days were full of magic and experiments. Fred, Violet and their son Herbert lived and played in Cavanagans, the forest pub with its ever-lively crowd. Herbert decided that the tree house should stay. He was almost as tall as his father, but they both felt they were not too old to enjoy such things. Herbert then found the perfect place inside it for his telescope. On clear evenings, they would both go up to the tree house, chat happily, enjoy each other's company and view the moon and stars.

There was a certain hour, after Cavanagans had closed, when Herbert was asleep, Violet would have just fallen into bed to sleep as deep as the dead and Fred would sit on the quiet terrace listening to the rise and fall of the leaves and the insects' night time chattering. In time, magic and science would pull up chairs and sit beside him in his thoughts. In the dark, with only lamplight around him, his mind turned to consider black hearts, biological evidence of bad intentions and his experiments to discern the physiological impact of actions persistently carried out with destructive intent. He would wrap up in a thick coat and knitted scarf with a mug or glass of something to warm him as the night drew in and his pensive expression told of the debates going on in his mind. Could the physical heart of a magician reveal the badness within? His experiments suggested it could. Could blood be polluted or corrupted by evil? Could it be cured, restored to health? What if something perceived as bad was actually good? Could the body discern the truth better than the mind? Could someone with a self-belief of infallible virtue have a heart as black as coal, without their knowledge? Or could the condemned, believing they are bad, actually have hearts as pure and clear as a mountain stream? He wanted to decode evil, break it down and reverse it.

Magic changes the heart. In the same way the birth of a child expands the heart, the development of one's magical capacity changes it physically, as well as one's belief and understanding of the world. Both the physical and psychological aspects interested him, but it was the physical elements he could test empirically. With magic and science collaborating he hoped to gain insights into both.

In magic creatures or individuals, when destructive thoughts dominate and the magic that results is born of fear, hate, jealousy, anger or such like the physical heart goes black. The more malevolent the intent, the greater the colouration and the longer it stays without reversal. Creatures with black hearts were hell bent on destruction and humans might be similar, Fred supposed, although they were more resourceful at concealing intent. Fred imagined that Raffaello Riviera, in his final moments, had a heart like polished black marble. He would have loved to have known for sure, but magic burn outs left no remnants for scientists to play with.

His best examples were with the living fish, whose bodies

he had lightened to transparency, which swam like cling-film creatures, their internal organs visible for inspection. Into the tank of gormless, gaping, but well-behaved guppies he would add a carefully selected fish, which he called a Bad-Freddie. A Bad-Freddie had the countenance and behaviour of a pike, with the elusiveness and blue lustre of a bastard fish. It would be found in a deep pool otherwise empty of life and with good reason. No chance of a Bad-Freddie going hungry, bellicose Bad-Freddie devoured others for the immediate taste of destruction. The scales of others were splattered, hanging from his sharp, thorny gills. From a life of such bullying and consumption the fish's stomach was over-extended and so when empty, felt like a void he must fill at all costs.

In the tank where the Bad-Freddie fish acquired transparency, smaller fish could soon be seen swimming bewilderedly through its digestive tract. Later they may be returned to their friends, but Fred was primarily concerned with observing the heart. The more the Bad-Freddie devoured and destroyed the darker the aquatic heart became. Blacker and blacker in line with his aggression and at a point, somewhere past the three quarter mark, it affected the fish's eyes. The eyes lost vitality, dulled, depth was reduced and they looked flatter, like dead eyes.

Fred came to recognise 'dead-eyes' whenever he saw them and he was always wary. He would usher small children away from the pedigree dog whose eyes looked so and he once watched with intrigue as a dead-eyed woman read a love poem at the wedding of her brother, her eyes sending a very different message.

To understand more he would have to do some gruesome work with exhumed bodies, which he did not relish. He would have to speak to the morgue and see what permissions could be granted for science with magic providing an invisible mending service for every suture he made. The thought of it repulsed him, but his curiosity overpowered him, he really wanted to learn more. To understand how good becomes bad, ultimately to be able to prevent it, for goodness to triumph.

Violet referred to his work as his 'explorations in evil'. She told him that he must secretly admire the Bad-Freddie to have named him so, that he must have a latent appetite for destruction. So he ensured that the transparent fish took on a lavender-blue tint whenever she arrived to watch and he enticed the Bad-Freddie to power round the tank in displays of bravado, jumping up and flashing her his dead eyes.

ESTHER VALENCIA'S FLOURISHES

*E*sther's Flourishes, which she thought of as serpents, were her proudest creation, although they were just magic with no shape or form. She invented them to help other magicians' work be the best it could be. They infiltrated other people's magic to meticulously refine the details and if necessary provide finishing flourishes in the style of the original creator. Esther liked order and rhythm and all loose ends tied up, without exception.

Even some of the greatest spells created by her best friend Violet and her husband Horatio were sometimes just a little too messy and often 'almost' or 'nearly' complete before being sent out into the world. Knowing Horatio, Violet and Fred incredibly well, she was able to do what Horatio mocked as 'a little tidying and polishing here and there' by sending out the Flourishes to make good and merge seamlessly with the magic of others. The 'wonderful weavers' Violet called them, as they threaded through existing magic creating order, filling gaps and straightening up.

Esther was good at reading other people's magic. The Valencia family, from which she had come, were skilled code breakers, almost equal in ability to the Savine family, who were the best in the land. She enjoyed taking apart magic codes, understanding and anticipating their patterns and the minds of their creators.

For many years Violet was unaware of the wonderful weavers at work in her magic. She would whoop with delight at the unexpected endings. 'Esther, look at that cascade of fireflies! What a perfect flourish!' she would say, watching, wide-eyed as they lit the sky. And so the serpents of Esther's mind found a name, the name that they would be known to the world as. Esther loved Violet's reactions; she did not have the heart to tell her that her Flourishes had created the effects, for fear of upsetting her. She also found great amusement in Violet's complete acceptance of any peculiarities as being things she must have done, but had forgotten or had come about by chance, 'Look at that Esther! Was that me? Brilliant!'

Horatio's magic was always ordered, but it was sometimes left unfinished. So Esther began softly, imperceptibly sending out Flourishes when she knew he was experimenting. They infiltrated his work without detection. It meant she would no longer be irritated by his unfinished spells and he could happily and mercurially jump from one magic idea to another. One day she had to come clean.

She should have never released the Flourishes whilst in a temper, but he had really annoyed her. His spell was a simple one, to create spectacular coloured masks that would transform to match the moods and characteristics of their wearers. Horatio wanted to have a picnic in the courtyard and play with them, but he was taking too long and besides, he had forgotten that it was her birthday. This was not a birthday picnic that he had organised. It was a picnic for the magic four and the visiting guest magicians. He had ordered a rich lemon cake to be made. She had tasted the icing in the kitchen, sharp and sweet.

Masks kept appearing everywhere. Tigers, cherubs, mallards, harlequins and before he had finished his thinking, all of the masks were complete, in neat rows, in his office, bright colours against the dark wood, floating in the air, waiting for him. The beautiful thing about Esther's Flourishes was that they understood his magic and his mind. He had been aiming for twenty masks and twenty there were, in designs that were very much his style, ideas he would have had, artistic choices he would have made if only he had had the chance. He looked up at them in disbelief. Esther was attending the flowers in the courtyard, yanking out coarse weeds with firm hands when she heard him stomping around and shouting, 'Esther! Esther! It's gone errant, it's all gone errant! Esther! My spell is thinking for itself! How could that happen? Esther!' His voice echoed around the stone walls.

She took a blousy pink rose, closed her eyes, and drank in its scent, the fragrance cheering her. He was still hollering. She decided to confess, after she had finished the watering, which would leave just the right amount of time for him to tread heavily and noisily through the whole of the castle before finding her.

He listened as she explained, sat up straight and bristled a little, but was impressed enough not to be annoyed. She watched the dark features of his face move from creased up indignation, softening in intense interest, to smooth out completely at the thought that her Flourishes could be applied to other people's magic. Realising that the somewhat slapdash and occasionally ridiculous spells that filled his home could be improved soothed him immediately. But his competitive nature never rested and he called it the 'tidying and polishing spell' as if its domestic label would reduce its magnificence. They would both smile at this little joke, knowing he was wrong.

Once Horatio knew, she had to tell the others. Violet thought it ingenious and hilarious how she had been outwitted. Fred did not laugh; he was staggered and she knew he regarded her differently from that day on. Respectful, as he always was, he would sometimes look at her oddly, then look away and she knew that he was thinking, 'devious, dark depths.' She could see it in his eyes. Neither Fred nor Violet nor Horatio could replicate Esther's Flourishes, so they called on her help when they needed it. Violet occasionally left deliberately incomplete spells, in tangible shimmering form, for Esther to trip up on as she got out of bed, which made both her and Esther smile in the mornings.

Esther had once seen a snake swim across a lagoon and had been mesmerised by its motion, the perfect S shape undulating and travelling forward. S for snake, as if it was writing its identity in the water and repeating it over and over with every movement it made. S for snake, S for snake, S for snake or S for Scion, Esther wondered.

PART II

Still twenty-five years before Annabelle Drake wrote her History of Stonerock Castle

NATHAN GLASS

*B*eyond the northern forest, beyond the wheat fields, the patchwork quilt of green hills and the winding woods is the small hamlet of Calamity. Its one pub and nine houses link to the three farms that converge at its centre. The Glass family have lived on the smallest farm for generations, breeding horses and growing chicory.

Nathan grew up galloping across dales, swimming in lakes and climbing cedar trees, immersed in nature. His days were punctuated by sunrise and sunset and his needs had always been simple. Until he realised he was different. The publican of the Prancing Peacock noticed it first; when Nathan was playing darts, he had an aim and an eye that were precision perfect. The publican would challenge all visitors to beat the young lad and he and Nathan would split their winnings when the visitors went home empty-handed.

Then his mother noticed it with the horses. The spooked ones, the timid ones, the unhinged and skittish ones all instantly let him ride. 'Skill' said his father. 'Special' said his mother.

When a fire broke out in the hay barn of a neighbouring

farm, tearing down two stories, they watched him ride across the fields towards the orange flames and watched them recede at the same speed that he advanced. The wild inferno, the crackling sounds and the pumping black smoke all stopped suddenly. As if some unseen water had doused the fire. Everything went eerily silent. The charcoaled remains of the barn lay dampened and crumpled. His horse padded around the wet ash, while the sun burned in the sky and the stinging taste of smoke hung in his throat.

'I put it out in my mind,' he replied when his father asked what had happened. His father shook his head and would not meet his mother's stare.

'If he is magic, we must not hold him back,' said his father.

'Matilda will run the farm,' said his mother referring to Nathan's younger sister who had always shown more interest and would be sure to keep the accounts as precision perfect as Nathan's darts. It was settled.

His parents had no magic friends or contacts, but were determined to help him. The Glass family were hardworking, with a lineage of formidable women and firm handed men. With an agreement that the darts competitions in the Prancing Peacock continued, each evening, the Glass family were able to charm or influence the visiting magicians to help their son make the best of the gifts he had been given. The back room of the pub, on creaking chairs, amidst the smells of spilled ale and beef stew heating in the kitchen, was where the conversations and subsequently the teachings took place. Lessons ended only when the sun rose to witness tired magicians staggering around with a large bag of chicory or falling asleep on a new horse as they returned home.

Nathan's mother was worried about the frauds and charlatans, who would waste their time. She need not have worried. Her son was good at spotting them; her husband good at ensuring they did not return.

Nathan enjoyed meeting the wild variety of magic folk who came to the pub. What they taught him beyond refinements to his magic was to believe completely in himself, that nothing would be impossible and to avoid double negatives in spells. They told him of the magic four and of the experiments at Stonerock castle. Nathan was six years younger than the magic four, but his pub-friends were adamant that his magic was equally as good. He must go and join them said the snake charmer, the grey-eyed hypnotist and the elderly lady who turned cherries into rubies.

Stonerock castle was a fairytale in Nathan's mind. He had rarely gone much further than the hamlet of Calamity and its surrounding countryside. He knew the story of Raffaello Riviera and the pictures of the castle and its eagles were drawn so beautifully in his mind that he could hardly imagine the place to exist anywhere other than in his head. He loved Raffaello's story, in spite of its tragic ending. He too had felt the isolation of magic and often tramped through the wheat fields imagining he was Raffaello pacing the corridors of the castle.

His mother realised that her son knew more than the crazy folk who came to the pub and sensed his growing frustration. Nathan returned home one morning to find that his bags were packed. His father looked serious and handed him a key.

'You must go to Escaville. There's a small house for you. You're to go to the castle and meet the magic four. Learn all you can. They're older, but don't be intimidated. The Scion is yet to be found.'

NATHAN LOOKED at himself in the mirror; wearing the brown tweed suit his grandmother had made for him many years before, a crisp white shirt and a thin red tie. He was not sure it was a tie at all, but he liked it and fastened it around his neck. It looked too feminine at first, so he tugged at it, pulling the ends this way and that, until it hung as he wanted it to. He smiled. This was how he wanted to look, to be himself, wearing something he felt comfortable in. He cared about what the magic four would think of him, but just as strong was his desire to be himself. If they accepted him, they would be accepting the true Nathan Glass. He ran his fingers through his hair to tidy it a little. It was time to go.

As he walked he felt as if he should be practising things in his mind. Several of the magicians in the pub had advised him to go through his 'repertoire of magic' if he was ever nervous. He did not tell them that he had yet to find a task or trick that he was unable to do. Their advice was of little comfort to him on the long walk through the vast southern forest. His repertoire was anything he set his mind to. It was that simple. Some things took longer than others, but all was achievable; at least that had been his experience so far.

Perhaps that would change. Perhaps his eyes would be opened to challenges beyond his imagination. He hoped with all his heart that he would have to work hard to keep up with the magic four. He wanted to feel intimidated by their greatness; as he knew that would bring relief as well as excitement. More than that he wanted to talk, to engage with people who knew what it was like to see the world in the way he did.

AT THE EDGE of the southern forest, on a high and wide promontory, set against a backdrop of the sea, stood an imposing stone castle. It had a raised portcullis and huge open doors that led to a vaulted entrance hall, filled with light. The entrance was mirrored by a stone archway inside, directly opposite, with doors that led out to the courtyard.

Three rather bewildered lavender flamingos lingered on the steps to the entrance as Nathan came out of the forest and made his way towards the castle.

'Go! Go! Be gone!' said a tall, thin man with glasses, his angular frame all the more pronounced as he ran towards them waving a large broom. 'You filthy, messy creatures!' They ran a few metres away, out of the reach of the broom. 'Damn things!' he said, as Nathan approached. Nathan smiled at the man. He grimaced as he looked at the ground. 'It's been a year since the Cavanagan wedding and they're still here. Excreting all over the entrance! Why Violet couldn't be happy with flowers, I'll never know.'

Nathan looked at the birds and made eye contact. They rose suddenly in a frenzy of lilac feathers and squawks and flew out to sea. 'Don't come back you dumb-brained defecators!' yelled the man.

'Nathan Glass,' said Nathan extending his hand to him.

'Salem. I just work here. The weird and wonderful are through there,' he said, gesturing towards the courtyard. 'You here to watch or participate?'

'Participate.'

Salem's face lit up and he pushed his glasses closer to his eyes to have a good look at Nathan.

'That will please them. They're getting a bit restless. Maybe you'll keep them occupied. Nothing more troublesome than a bored magician.'

'Are the magic four inside?'

Salem's face lit up again.

'Horatio will like you. People have started calling them the two families. He likes the magic four better. Esther Valencia is not a Drake yet!' Salem drifted off in thought, before snapping back into action with the broom, its bristles sweeping brusquely against the stone. 'In you go.'

. . .

NATHAN WOULD THINK BACK to that day, to his reflection in the glass, to the odd tie, the smell of jasmine and honey. He was alive with hope, glowing with optimism. He remembers that image as the time when he was pure. A young man in a brown tweed suit, untainted. When destiny was a hunched figure, beckoning to him with a crooked finger and a squinting eye. He ran obediently towards it with all the hunger of youth and limbs that longed to power forward and leave everything behind.

NATHAN ENTERED the vaulted hall and stood under the stone archway looking through at a world full of colour. People glanced up from their activities in the bright light of the courtyard and the shaded walkways. He took a deep breath and walked in. Flowers were being created on the castle wall. They arrived in bursts of mauve and yellow, the scent of jasmine filling the air. To his immediate right three young men were experimenting with its perfume and formation, making it climb higher and faster. He watched the green tendrils grow and expand like splayed fingers climbing up the stone and as each bud opened more fragrance escaped. He smiled. An elegant woman sitting in the shade applauded their work and as she did so, small iridescent coloured birds flew out from her hands and landed on the foliage.

To his left a man and a woman were pushing the space between them with considerable force, as if they held an invisible object between them. A game, working back and forward with their magic, feet slipping on the grass, losing a shoe, each receding and gaining ground in turn, determined and focused, faltering when they stopped to laugh or curse.

A smoky pink explosion occurred in the centre of the courtyard and a huge muddy elephant suddenly appeared. Thrilled, people ran to it. Its solidity became ghost-like when they reached to touch it and their hands fell through the air. A quick magic response, in playful competition, cleaned up the elephant and saddled him with a crocheted coat, which another's magic removed as quickly as it had appeared. Then a triumphant looking man jumped and sat on top of the now solid elephant, which gave a bemused trumpet in response. Nathan looked around, eager to guess which action was carried out by whom, torn between working it out and watching the continuing spectacle. As the elephant raised its trunk and sprayed water over its back, the man fell down and sprung back on his hands like an acrobat. The whole image dissolved into colourful rain, which sank into the lush grass. People cheered and bursts of water hit the man from different directions. He bowed wet and smiling.

The large courtyard had lawns, fountains and gardens set within it. Nathan found a space to sit on the grass. He felt the sun on his face, listened to the trickling water and observed all that was around him. Two elderly gentlemen before him were transforming their faces into those of brown bears. They stood opposite each other, acting as mirrors to each other's work, critiquing harshly and laughing. Their amusement was infectious, yet they were serious too. With precision they faded from human to bear, minute change by minute change. The bones and muscles of each face slowly neatened in definition through meticulously detailed magic. They paused with their faces mid-bear, mid-human; pleased with the look, they sat down to share nectarines and honey sandwiches.

Nathan recognised Elspeth, a petite, elderly woman, who had taught him how to create anti-venom and stronger force fields than he had yet accomplished, invisible walls for protection or entrapment. She had left The Prancing Peacock with a bag of chicory as big as she was and a bottle of navy rum. She whistled, grinned and waved at him. She was standing next to a bright yellow, upright creature who looked part dragon. He was absentmindedly blowing out small rings of flames, tiny burning halos that floated up like bubbles. Nathan noticed a few more odd looking creatures and was unsure if they were the result of magic play, cursed or naturally peculiar. He supposed that it did not matter.

A small boy ran up to Nathan.

'You'll do,' he said with a winning smile. Then he held up a rock, jagged at the top, rounded at the bottom. 'Please sir, can you magic me one more like this? It will help me so much, I want them to be exactly the same.'

Nathan put out his palm; the boy gave him the rock.

'What is it for?' said Nathan, closing his hand and feeling the rock's coolness, its rough and smooth textures.

'For my model. A two headed monster! I've made their necks from amber beads and this stone balances perfectly, but I need them to be exactly the same.' The boy hopped around in enthusiasm.

'Tricky,' said Nathan smiling.

'Mum had a go, but she couldn't do it.'

He looked disappointed as Nathan handed him back the stone. The boy closed his palm and then jumped in surprise. He opened his hand again to see an identical stone had appeared next to the first.

'Yes!' he shouted, his eyes filled with happiness and he bounced around in excitement. Nathan smiled. The boy ran across the courtyard and yelled, 'Thank you!' over his shoulder.

Nathan felt he had come to a place he had been homesick for his whole life. He felt so peaceful that he could have lain on the soft grass and fallen into a deep sleep, but his curiosity kept him alert and he was intrigued to see the outcomes of the experiments around him.

On the other side of the courtyard, still fidgeting with

excitement, the small boy handed Frederick Cavanagan the two stones.

'He did it!' beamed the boy. Violet Cavanagan turned towards Nathan. Fred clasped the stones between his hands and pressed them together, closing his eyes as if in prayer. 'But it's just rocks, right? It's not like he created a fire dragon or an elephant in pink smoke is it?' said the boy. Fred was hardly listening. Violet put her arm around the boy and said,

'Sometimes it's the little things that are tricky, especially when there is more than meets the eye within the rock. Your rock is ore, full of precious things, so small you cannot see them all, only glimmers of some. Beautiful. A great choice for a monster's head. I know exactly where in the southern forest you would have found it.'

The boy's jaw dropped. 'But I have no intention of telling your parents. You were brave to venture in so far.'

'397 minerals. All there, in exact quantities,' said Fred opening his eyes, looking surprised and pleased.

'And cut?'

'Perfect. Exact. He's good.'

Fred gave the stones to the boy who grinned and ran off to complete his monster.

From a distance Violet looked over at Nathan and smiled. Most magicians who came to the castle were nervous, sometimes ridiculously defensive or needing constant reassurance. Such interactions bored her immensely. Nathan's relaxed form and his highly accomplished magic filled her with excitement. She rubbed her hands together.

'Horatio will love him!' she said to Fred.

'Horatio will hate him,' Fred replied.

A loud peal of bells sounded abruptly, making people jump and breaking their concentration. A fair haired woman, who had been blowing on the roses to deadhead them, stood up, silenced the courtyard and said pleasantly, but firmly,

'All sound work in the forest today please,'

She then returned to her work. Nathan's eyes widened when he saw her. She was truly beautiful, her eyes full of vitality, her movements graceful yet purposeful. He did not think she had noticed him and he watched her inquisitively. He noticed that she was putting things right in the rose garden with great care and attention, a tapping of her fingers here, a flick of her wrist there, movements hardly perceptible, but each with an action and intention. He discerned that she could transform the whole garden in an instant, if she chose, but she chose not to. She let nature be and worked alongside it, sure and decisive. A respect for what nature created was bedded deep in his heart and he was drawn to this woman in ways both profound and inexpressible. He could not tear his eyes away, the pale smoothness of her skin, cheeks with rosy apple glow and the confident gestures of her elegant hands. He noticed an unusual ring on her finger, a figure of eight encasing two large yellow stones.

'She's one of the magic four,' said Elspeth from the Prancing Peacock who had sidled up next to Nathan. 'She's my favourite too.' They watched her select two roses and cut them. She then straightened up and walked over to them smiling graciously. She extended her hand and introduced herself,

'Esther Valencia.'

One after the other Elspeth and Nathan shook her hand and took the flower she offered them, both of them delighted, fumbling and awkward.

'Horatio Drake,' said a broad, athletic man, with supreme confidence, who was now standing before them and whose arrival Nathan had completely missed. Horatio shook their hands. Elspeth's arm and shoulder flapped from such a firm greeting. Horatio stared at Nathan with penetrating brown eyes, dragging Nathan's thoughts away from Esther.

'Now, tell me Elspeth, is he any good?' asked Horatio.

'He's the one I've been telling you about! From Calamity,' she replied.

Horatio raised his eyebrows in acknowledgement and broke into a huge smile.

THE MAGIC FIVE

*V*iolet was walking and talking at speed and Nathan was trying to keep up as they walked across the courtyard. She stopped abruptly, gave a brief request to Salem who was cleaning the lanterns, before going through a side door into the Castle. Nathan waited outside and imagined her continuing to walk and talk without registering that he was no longer with her. Salem watched him, hesitating to enter the castle uninvited, with a smile. Nathan stood staring at the closing door. The men, women and creatures experimenting close by discreetly waited to see what he would do. They had never been invited inside, were relieved by his uncertainty and secretly enjoyed his discomfort.

Salem looked across to the other side of the courtyard to get Horatio's attention, but he was already striding towards them, breaking into a light run. Nathan put his hands in his pockets and shifted from one foot to another.

'You came back,' Horatio said, pleased.

'Yes. Violet wanted me to help her with something.'

'Oh dear,' Horatio replied. His eyes were bright and alert as he looked at Nathan, who smiled nervously and looked around in apprehension, actions which Horatio keenly observed. He looked at Nathan in fascination, before gesturing to the door and saying, 'after you.' The courtyard fell silent. Salem grinned widely and swung open the door. Nathan stepped in. When they were both inside Horatio hesitated. Nathan waited for him to speak. There was an uncomfortably long pause, and then Horatio looked suddenly perturbed and said,

'You must excuse me. I have to finish something, but feel free to look around, Violet will be in here somewhere. I'm sure you'll find her.' He quickly strode up a staircase almost breaking into a run. Nathan was left alone, confused, listening to the fading echo of his footsteps, wondering if Horatio had immediately regretted letting him in. He was unsure of which direction to take, so he stood looking about him at the paintings on the walls.

Soon, a large tower of boxes came wobbling its way along the corridor, the face of its owner hidden behind them. Only the feet that were cautiously making their way without the guidance of sight were visible beneath a long skirt and elegant hands holding the box at the bottom. Nathan recognised the unusual ring on the right hand, two large vivid stones, encased with diamonds. He felt a wild happiness racing around inside as he sprang into action.

'Esther, let me help you.'

'Oh, hello! It's you,' she replied.

'Yes, Horatio invited me.'

He removed the top boxes, so that she could see. Her grey eyes lit up and she smiled.

'Thank you.'

For a moment he froze. Her bright smile made his thoughts spin too quickly for him to hold onto them. She looked at him. He looked down.

'Um, that is an amazing ring. Beautiful.'

Esther looked pleased.

'Sapphires. Yellow Sapphires,' she said as they both studied them. The twin stones were set vertically, in a swirling figure of eight, sparkling, 'Precious cats' eyes!' she said and laughed.

Nathan looked up and she continued, a playful look in her her eyes. 'Stolen from an ancient tomb. Eyes plucked out of a stone cat, who was set to guard her mistress's burial chamber and the treasures she took to the grave. The robbers approached the statue from behind and took the eyes so that the cat would not see them, as they destroyed the grave and took the gold and jewels. But the next day they were all found dead. Scratches all over their faces.' Esther's eyes glinted with mischief and Nathan smiled at her story.

'And how is it that you have the sapphire eyes?'

She laughed. 'Griswald Goat, Horatio's godfather, left them to me when he died. They were wrapped in a bandage, inside a letter written in calligraphic script, telling the tale of the cat.'

'Do you believe it?'

'Not really, but I loved his imagination and his spelling mistakes and his attempt to draw the cat. It's my favourite piece of jewellery.'

She pushed open a large door that had been set ajar and he followed her in.

'Be careful of the spheres down there,' she said, 'these are the last ones.'

The floor was covered with what looked like large marbles, about the size of tennis balls, the insides varying in shape and colour. Nathan placed the boxes down on a side table, picked one of the spheres up and looked at it curiously. It was full of moving images. He looked at Esther open-mouthed.

'What are these?' he asked.

'Dream spheres. These are new to you! Oh how wonderful. They are a sensational use of magic. Violet and I have days of fun creating these. She cut a hole in the sky and found another world; which almost caused her to accidentally burn out, poor thing, but now we have access to it and we are going to send out dream spheres for fun and scientific purpose.'

'Another world?'

'Yes! Don't tell anyone. And don't get too excited, there is no magic beyond what nature creates over there. People have been there before, for books; I remember my grandmother telling me about such a place, but I had no idea how to get there. Violet has created a permanent gateway. Horatio goes through to pick up music scores and poetry, brings back a new library each time. He's not so keen on making the spheres. He liked the idea for about five minutes, made one sphere and got bored. The people over there need cheering up, so that is what we have been doing. Violet and I are creating all kinds of hilarity. You can help us. Let me show you how to make one.'

One month after Nathan first arrived at the castle

'ESTHER HAS AMAZING EYES,' said Nathan, leaning against the stone wall.

'Really,' replied Salem non committally.

'Like a calm sea, when sunlight reflects on it, in the late afternoon. Grey against a backdrop of faded blue. Vivid without vivid colour, like twilight. Glowing like the moon's reflection in a lake, silvery bright.'

Nathan seemed to completely disappear into his thoughts. Salem mused that he was hardly present at all.

'A lake silvery bright, eh?' said Salem in mild amusement.

Nathan did not hear. Salem's smile vanished when he saw Horatio headed their way. Nathan had not seen him, which amazed Salem, who wondered how anyone could miss him as he bounded around the courtyard like a gorilla. Nathan was skating on lakes silvery bright, Salem thought, as Horatio reached them.

'What are you two talking about?' Horatio asked.

'The colour of Esther's eyes,' said Salem impassively, allowing Nathan a second or so to jolt out of his reverie and appear similarly unmoved. Horatio placed his hand across his chin and thought for a moment.

'Brown? No, grey. Blue. I should know; they stare so adoringly at me. What's for lunch? You staying Nathan?' asked Horatio.

Two Months Later

'I NEED NATHAN. He'll be good at this,' said Violet, laughing as she entered the room where Fred, Horatio and Nathan sat in the blue velvet chairs. Fred was reading and looked up from his book. Horatio was in animated flow talking to Nathan and did not pause.

'What are you up to?' asked Fred, raising an eyebrow in playful suspicion.

'I'm designing something good. Come, come Nathan,' said Violet.

Nathan smiled at her, but he was still listening to Horatio who had failed to acknowledge Violet's interruption as an interruption. She stared at Nathan with a mixture of mischievousness and impatience, vying for his attention. Horatio's sentence showed no sign of stopping. Nathan looked repeatedly from one to the other. Fred put his book down and watched them in amusement.

'Come on Nathan!' said Violet.

Horatio turned suddenly to look at her and let out a long, exaggerated sigh of frustration. Fred laughed. Violet laughed and grabbed Nathan's hand. 'We'll be no time at all Horatio. I will bring him back to you.'

THEY NESTLED in the small tea room, tucked away on the west side of the castle. Its entrance set into wooden panelling and only visible if you knew where to look. It was the only interior designed by Cecelia Riviera that was truly welcoming. The white ceiling was piped like delicious icing and the silk wallpaper in coral-pink and gold had a delicate warmth. The chairs, unique and inviting, were cosseted and buttoned in sumptuous layers of carefully chosen fabric and stood like children lovingly wrapped up before braving the cold. Violet sat happily with Nathan and Esther, all three in a chair that would become their favourite.

'Now that I've got you both,' began Violet.

'Look at that face,' Esther said, addressing Nathan as she indicated to Violet, 'remember it. Learn it. It means there's no stopping her.'

'What do you mean? I am here to delight you!' said Violet.

'Surrender now. You can't stop the tide. Any plans you had for this morning Nathan, gone.'

'Will this take long? Horatio still wants to speak to me.'

'No. Of course not,' said Violet.

Esther laughed.

'It will take as long as it takes,' Violet added. 'We'll call it 'civil engineering for the mind'. We'll meet here each week. If we call it play Esther will get restless and won't stay long. If we call it something that Horatio will find interesting he will be in here and we'll never get rid of him. He is too competitive to enjoy this.'

'That's true,' said Esther.

Violet reached behind a cushion and took out a small book crudely covered in damask wallpaper, bound with ageing adhesive tape. Esther brightened at the sight of it.

'I want you to close your eyes,' said Violet. Both obeyed. 'I am going to read you a description of the waheehaa bird.'

'I love Griswald Goat's stories,' said Esther, opening her eyes.

'Esther close your eyes,' said Violet.

'We must let Nathan read them,' Esther added.

'I would like you to create a dream sphere and place inside it the waheehaa bird and nothing more. I want to see what you see. I'll do it too and then we'll take a look. Here we go:

His mane like petals dark and bright,
His eyes a tempest in eerie light,
His curtain feathers of boiling rage,
His coat tails jagged, green as sage,
But legs so dandy, pink and sweet,
With hairy ankles and thunderstorm feet.'

Then came the beautiful silence as they focused, their smiles fading gently, their concentration deepening as they worked.

'I see him so clearly with those thunderstorm feet,' said Esther eventually. They all opened their eyes and held up their transparent dream sphere, containing the image of the waheehaa bird that had appeared before them. They passed them round.

'I like yours!'

'Oh, I like yours!'

'Yours is much scarier!'

'Nathan, that's truly terrifying,' said Violet.

'Now *those* are thunderstorm feet!'

They passed the spheres round and round, enlarging them from their original form, to take a better look. The three peculiar birds, all dramatically different, suspended in the large bubble-like globes, made them laugh.

'Shall we set them free?' said Nathan, his eyes lit with daring.

'Not your one, look at that vicious beak. We wouldn't stand a chance!' said Esther.

'My one looks quite gracious. If only we could!' said Violet.

'If only we could!' said Esther.

They both looked at Nathan. They were testing him and he knew it. He was pleased and struggled to contain his smile. Slowly, deliberately, he picked up the spheres.

'They look so baffled,' he said, as the birds turned and looked out, eyes wide and beaks open as if suddenly conscious of their spheres and the world around them. They pecked at their spheres as if to hatch. In an instant, the spheres were gone and three squawking waheehaas strutted around the floor. Nathan reached out to ruffle the maroon, petal-like mane of his creation.

'Ahh! How did you do that?' asked Esther.

'Do what?' asked Nathan smiling.

'Yes!' said Violet beaming.

'Amazing. Can I keep mine?' said Esther.

'They are illusions still. My one is quite friendly, he just looks merciless,' said Nathan.

'Illusions that you can touch and hear,' said Esther.

'And smell. That acrid, hen house smell,' said Violet, sniffing at her bird's feathers.

The three birds noticed each other, formed an orderly line, stared long and hard at their creators, circled them, shook their thunderstorm feet, then strutted towards the door, which opened to let them out.

'Oh, Salem will be after you!' cried Esther.

'They'll last until they see his scowl, then they'll vanish without trace,' said Nathan. They all laughed wickedly in anticipation.

AND SO THE three met each week in the small and pretty room where Cecelia Riviera had once entertained only her most favourite guests. They imagined and created dream spheres and took it in turns to look at the results. Sometimes Nathan would bring one of their creations into the room for entertainment. They had three favourites: the dappled sunlight of sitting under a great oak, a Cavalier King Charles spaniel and a towering castle of dark chocolate with gargoyles of dark fudge whose eyes were raspberry fruitlets. The lighting, the cake and the dog appeared most weeks. They devoured the cake and sucked out the gargoyles' eyes. It all tasted so rich and real but Nathan assured them it was merely illusion, a delicious illusion. The spaniel that joined them for the meetings sat happily in their laps, his soft ears soothing to stroke. He disappeared when each session was called to a close, and was always overjoyed to see them when one of them would re-imagine him the following week.

One week Nathan brought with him a sphere that showed them the meadows of Calamity as he remembered them as a child. He broke the sphere open. Violet and Esther closed their eyes and the images filled their minds.

They became young girls; instantly caught in the exhilaration of running through a world of green. They pelted across the landscape; through the rushing grass, their skin tingling as it skimmed their legs. Grass flecked with poppy red and cornflower blue, vast as the sea. Eventually, as they slowed, they came towards a sun drenched field and the scent of freshly cut grass. On reaching it they twirled with their arms open, against the backdrop of bright blue sky and mountain. They fell, laughing, to lie on the fresh, fragrant ground, warm and soft, closing their eyes with the sun on their faces. They revelled in this memory that their friend had spun into a dream.

They woke after a few moments, but with the satisfaction of having spent a full summer's day in a place of immense beauty. Violet requested vast quantities of copies, to send out through the Waiting Room, to combat the misery; her charity work, she explained to him. Esther said she could not remember ever feeling so free. She looked so dreamily happy and beautiful that silent fireworks of joy exploded inside Nathan. It gave him an idea of something he could make for Esther. A private project, to tinker with every now and then; an outlet for all he felt and thought about her. Maybe one day, if he felt brave, he would give it to her.

They travelled each week to places in their memories and imaginations and to mix-muddled places that were a little of each; with a dash of a story once told, part forgotten and a pinch of something once read. They would continue their day with cheerful expressions, relaxed shoulders and a fondness for everyone they encountered, at least for the first thirty minutes.

One Month Later

HORATIO HAD LET Fred's 'fishy magic' experiments accumulate in a large section of the third floor of the castle. He had been intrigued by Fred's findings, enjoyed having his friend close by and liked to feel he was a patron of important and worldly things. Nathan was also interested in Fred's experiments. When Horatio took him up to Fred's lab he walked around in fascination, stopping here and there to watch the fish. His keenness pleased Horatio. Fred observed Horatio's satisfied expression and remembered Violet's remark at breakfast:

'Horatio is a little transfixed by Nathan, wanting to show him the world, even sharing his grand and important toys. I think he might give Nathan the moon should he ask for it.'

'Well, I'm not complaining,' Fred had replied, 'this is the best mood he has been in for years and he is interrupting me less and less.'

Nathan asked Fred considered questions about his work on black hearts. His interest animated Fred, whose thoughts and theories spilled out in gushes of enthusiasm. They concluded that the experiments needed to be done on a greater scale and that they should work together. This thought was completely thrilling to both of them.

'Now I DID HAVE a Fred once; I think he may have wandered off into your castle and I have not seen him for some time,' said Violet loudly as Esther came into Cavanagans and sat on a bar stool. Violet smiled and handed Esther a blue drink in a long glass.

'He's working with Nathan. They are making great progress and are zipping round like naughty school boys, moving things, demanding things. Horatio is getting frazzled. He's secretly aghast at their prolonged enthusiasm,' said Esther.

'Progress?' Violet asked.

'Yes. Why the creature becomes focused on destruction remains unexplained, a variety of reasons most probably. However, they have more evidence that the darker the heart goes the more physical changes in the body can be observed.

They believe, and this is interesting to me, that the creature can feel its heart going black, the darkness in the blood in the moments that the change takes place.'

'How can they know what it feels?'

'I knew you would ask that. So you need to come over. I'm guessing heart rate changes, stress response, but how do they know for sure that it can feel it? They are supposing based on its reactions, I guess, but we can find out. They constructed a new aquarium, which we might like to experiment with, apparently,' said Esther.

'Oooh. And what about the white speck on the heart? Tell me it stays, because I don't need their experiments to tell me that it's there. I know it's there. There is always an incorruptible part. There must be.'

'But is there evidence?' Esther said grinning.

'Tell me!'

'Human observation suggests that in 75% of cases it is visible, decreasing in size and never static, but there was always the 25%. Fred had been working to look deeper into the flesh of the heart to find it. They managed that together and found it in the depths of 20%. So the elusive dark 5% remained, until yesterday. It is present and can only be seen through a different frequency of vision. It cannot be seen through the human eye. I gave them a list of two hundred suggestions. I do not know how many different frequencies they tried, I don't think they've slept for three days and they were using their own eyes for the frequency changes, so they must have cracking headaches.'

'But it's there!'

'Yes, but is the speck incorruptible or is it the agent of evil?'

'What do you mean?' Violet asked, intrigued.

'Is the speck the last bastion of goodness or is it the white agent killing off the goodness in the other cells? Your white speck might be the like the luminescence of the angler fish!'

'The white speck being at the centre of the destruction? No. Well, now I don't know,' said Violet.

'Good and bad, right and wrong; not always as easy to distinguish as one thinks, sometimes they look the same.'

'Hmm. Like mushrooms... or magicians,' Violet mused, smiling. 'One day we will know how evil forms. Then we can reverse it. My instinct tells me there is always goodness somewhere. There must be.'

Esther's eyes sparkled and she gave a wicked laugh,

'That's exactly what evil wants you to believe! That it is not pure. For then it can always lure you towards it, pull you closer and hold on to you,'

Violet's jaw dropped momentarily and her eyes widened before she smiled.

'No! Redemption is the unstoppable force,' she replied.

'Maybe. Clever Fred though. He is ecstatic and Nathan has been gracious in side stepping any credit and lauding Fred's work, although he too played a significant part.'

'As did you.'

'Yes. We work as a team. The fabulous five.'

They raised their glasses, 'Shall we go and play with the aquarium?'

'Yes. Let's go. Closing time everyone!' Violet swung herself over the counter to sit on it, 'Last one to finish locks up. Back later!'

'AT LAST CAVANAGAN, at last! And Esther you'll love this!' bellowed Horatio as the women approached the castle. He had been waiting for them and only knew how to wait impatiently. He raced down to greet them, stood in between them and interlaced his arms into theirs. 'I have something to show you,' he said smiling, his eyes sparkling in anticipation. He walked them into the castle, down the corridors to the doors of the great hall, trying hard to contain his excitement. Then stood before them and said, 'I humbly welcome you to Stonerock Aquarium,' and threw the doors open.

Esther took Horatio's hand and held it tightly. She took great pleasure in his enthusiasm and adored him, although he was a difficult man to love. In these moments it did not seem to matter. The door opened to a wall of water, a space completely filled, all sound muted. Before them was an underwater world of lightly swaying coral and seaweed either side of a pathway through the sand. A yellow fish swam past them at eye level and more flickers of colourful fins darted across their peripheral vision. Nathan came walking with Fred along the path, still working, as the faint pastel colours of the coral became more apparent and more fish appeared. They looked to the open doorway of new arrivals, smiled and beckoned. Fred's voice cut through the water in crystal clear sound:

'Come in, come and see.'

Horatio, Violet and Esther stepped into the warm, welcoming water. To their astonishment they remained dry and moved freely, able to breathe normally.

'Amazing,' said Violet and everyone heard her clearly. Violet took off her shoes to walk barefoot. Esther swam to a coral cave where black fish darted in and out. The new arrivals happy and awestruck played and examined the world that had been created, hardly speaking, but with expressions that were better than any praise. For Nathan and Fred watching their response was reward enough.

Fred and Nathan sat on the bottom of their underwater world counting and watching the fish and the rhythmic motion of an octopus above them. They had a fish, with a heart turning black in a cage, ready for release. They were tired. They looked at each other with understanding, with the same instinct, to enjoy the peace and the thought that the release could wait. They lay back. Fred was asleep in seconds. Nathan fought sleep. His eyes kept closing, but Esther was smiling and he wanted to see. Her laugher rang out as he drifted away, the sweetest of sounds, the happy song that permitted his slumber.

Two Months Later

HORATIO AND NATHAN stood at the top of the East Tower and looked out to sea. On the battlement walkway Nathan always thought of Raffaello Riviera. The story was easy to forget when enjoying the parties in the great hall or experiments in the courtyard, but with the cold sea breeze and the isolation of looking far out to sea, Nathan was always reminded of the castle's past. Raffaello and the storm, like fairytale images, appeared before his distracted gaze, accompanied by an unshakable sinking feeling. It made him uncomfortable and he wanted to leave.

Horatio enjoyed being at the top of the castle, watching the activity below and feeling a sense of pride in what belonged to him and what he was able to share. He found the sea breezes invigorating, even in winter. So they spent hours walking round the battlements, talking, discussing magic and challenging each other on how things should be done, Nathan with his collar turned up, losing all feeling in his extremities; their discussions and the warmth of their growing friendship making it bearable.

Horatio gave Nathan a winter scarf of his, a gift from Esther. Luxuriously soft silk, woven like tweed, olive and cinnamon colours with a flash of bronze running through it. It suited Nathan's complexion, his amber eyes. It looked better on Nathan than on it did on Horatio. Horatio conceded this and noted that he felt momentary jealousy without any resentment. He liked what he saw, the colours worked optimally, all was pleasing to the eye. Nathan should have a suit made in those colours, Horatio thought and made a mental note to inform his tailor.

Horatio wanted the castle to be a meeting place for magic minds. Nathan's presence had been a welcome relief from the fripperies of some of the minor magic regulars: Waftey Wheeler creating a new repulsively fragranced fern, some idiot filling the courtyard with rabbits in rainbow colours, the wisdom of philosophical reptiles; all these things had become trite. Horatio would have been as elated as Nathan about his arrival if it were not for a tiny niggling concern. Easily dismissed at this stage, but Horatio did not want it to grow, because Horatio could only be happy if he thought he was clearly ahead, the front runner for the Scion, successor of Raffaello. The fact that the castle had come to him, the seat of power had fallen into his lap, as if it was meant to be, gave him reassurance. He wanted Nathan to be brilliant, but not better.

At that moment with the sea air mild and restorative to him, the crash of the waves pleasing to his ear, Horatio looked at Nathan's profile, his alert eyes and felt hugely grateful that magic existed, that Nathan was here. He watched him smile, the tip of his nose and cheeks were pink with cold set against the vivid blue sky. He thought that Nathan was beautiful, or that women would find him beautiful, he corrected himself.

*H*oratio and Nathan were sitting in the shaded walkway at the edge of the courtyard, watching magicians experimenting with smoke and mild explosions in the sunlit garden. Horatio was supervising the creation of walls and smokescreens and a magical labyrinth was appearing before them, created by eager-eyed teenagers. Swirls of ghostly shapes drifted across the grass, interspersed with bursts of crackling metallic sparks. Nathan was keeping him company and occasionally reducing the volume of the overzealous ones. The air was crisp, the sun bright and the dust from each explosion caught like tiny blizzards in its rays.

'So, you are teaching now?' Nathan asked.

'Hmm. I suppose I am. Life lessons. Foresight, planning, military precision, pride in accuracy. Whatever they use the magic for, entertainment or survival, I want them to do it well. Poorly crafted spells reflect badly on us all. These kids were terrible. I saw them practicing and it irritated me so much that I brought them back here to show them how. They are coming along nicely now.'

'That's so very generous of you Horatio,' Nathan laughed.

'I thought so,' said Horatio smiling. 'They will learn how to impress others too. That's what they really want, to be impressive and adored.'

'To fall in love,' said Nathan.

'Maybe, for the lucky ones.'

'Like you with Esther, incredibly lucky.'

'Lucky?' mused Horatio, 'I am impressive and adored,' he said with a smile.

'Do you love her?' Nathan asked.

As soon as the question left his mouth, he was stunned

that he had actually asked it. Nathan had held the question, unsaid, for so long. He felt nervous now, as if he had released the safety pin on a grenade. He kept his emotions contained. Horatio leant back and said,

'Esther is a soft breeze on a summer's day, sunlit golden hair, the scent of a rose. She is everything that is wonderful: beauty, harmony and pleasantness. She can't be faulted. But sometimes I long for bad weather, its power, and its force, the crashing of the waves against the rock. I fear I will get bored, that her softness is not what I need, that I will become restless and difficult and unworthy of her.'

Horatio had never spoken so openly and honestly about his feelings before. He surprised both himself and Nathan. Nathan sat silently, absorbing this revelation and looking at the ground. Horatio watched the magicians working, whilst at marvelling at the clarity of his own expression. The smoke walls before them changed through a sequence of mesmerising colours and textures. Then Nathan sat up straight and turned to face Horatio. Horatio recoiled in surprise at the intensity of Nathan's stare.

'You don't love her,' Nathan snapped.

At first Horatio froze, like a child caught out. Then he laughed, shaking his head,

'Who knows? Can we talk about something else?'

'No. Beyond the softness there is something strong and solid. For the things that are important to her, she will weather any storm. She is the wall that wind and waves will rage against and never break. It's not weakness. She is all power, but it is so beautifully concealed that all you feel is the summer breeze.'

'Maybe,' Horatio replied, his expression tight.

'Maybe you should have married Violet.'

'Ha! That tempest would sink me,' he smiled and laughed nervously. 'No. Esther is the closest to what I want, but something holds me back.' His smile faded. He sat up, looking at Nathan with equal intensity, 'You seem to have thought a lot about Esther.'

'I adore her Horatio, but I know that she's yours and that she adores you, despite your ambivalence and procrastination. If I were you I would not hesitate. She is amazing, all anyone could ever want.'

Horatio's face darkened, his eyes lit fiercely,

'You romantic fool!' He replied, unable to mask his contempt; all joviality lost as he spat the words out. Nathan sat silently, remaining calm as Horatio glared at him in anger. Anger transformed Horatio's face, all its warmth gone, the dark features hardened. Unafraid, but still taken aback Nathan waited for him to speak, for his fury to be released. But instead Horatio stood abruptly and swept away, the unspent storm still raging inside him.

THE MAGIC FOUR

Two Days Later

*H*oratio was already in the room as the remaining four walked in. There were only four chairs at the table. Frederick noticed the missing velvet chair immediately and went to get another. Horatio greeted everyone except Nathan, who observed him, but did not try to get his attention. Horatio's characteristic exuberance had drained away. He was pale and distant. Esther reached out, touched his arm, but he hardly noticed. He stood looking out of the window staring at the frosted ground with green shoots pushing through, then at the trees in the distance that were coming into leaf. The others sat down at the table.

'They say Raffaello knew he was the greatest magician of his time, even though there was no way of knowing for certain, no way of comparing scientifically his power to that of other magic,' said Horatio turning round, looking at everyone except Nathan.

'Well, magic is more art than science, he could never know through accurate measures of data!' Violet replied, reclining in her chair.

'No, I disagree. I think we just haven't worked out how to measure it yet,' Horatio said.

'And why would we want to?' she replied.

'So we can understand everything,' he answered.

'Or we could just enjoy everything! Everything that magic gives us.'

Violet beamed at him, but Horatio shook his head impatiently.

'I wonder if the greatest magician is really going to be one of us, one of the magic four?' he asked. There was a hard edge to his voice. He looked again at everyone at the table except Nathan. It was clear to the others that Nathan had fallen from favour for some, as yet, indiscernible reason. Violet and Esther exchanged concerned glances. Out of Horatio's eye line Fred shot Nathan a consolatory smile and a friendly shrug of confusion. In Horatio's mind it was the magic four again and always would be. The brief interlude of five was a mistake, an inaccuracy that he was going to correct. Horatio sat down. Fred leaned in towards him.

'So you are wondering if it is you?' asked Fred.

'Yes, I have wondered. It is possible after all,' Horatio replied.

'As much as I want to mock your arrogance, I have wondered too. If it is me, not you, obviously,' said Violet. Horatio looked at her.

'Well, popular opinion suggests it will be you or I.'

Esther rolled her eyes, her face alight with mock fury.

'So you think Fred, Nathan and I are merely the runners up? According to your measures. Do you not see that we excel in power and style?' she said, banging the table loudly, then sitting back and smiling.

'We have more grace and poise and our execution is aesthetic perfection!' added Fred, gesturing widely and lavishly with his arms, then putting his feet on the table, lacing his hands behind his head. Even Horatio managed a weak smile.

'And what if Horatio is wrong?' asked Esther, looking at Fred and Nathan.

'Well I've never really considered myself, but now you have me wondering,' said Fred.

'I wonder too,' said Esther, rising and adopting a dramatic stance of power, 'what do you think, Nathan? Do I look like the greatest magician of our time?'

He smiled, 'No.'

She gasped and her face dropped in theatrical dismay. He did not take his eyes from her. She looked back at him as he said, 'No Esther, you are aesthetic perfection.'

Esther smiled, more in disbelief than pleasure and no one dared to look in Horatio's direction. The pause, the silence, rang through the room. Until eventually Fred coughed, a nervous convulsion, perhaps a distraction to kill the silence that he felt keenly or to stop Nathan from continuing. But Nathan continued, 'Like a melody that takes you away somewhere better, somewhere free. It's not the mere beauty of the notes, although they are beauty personified, but it's the power, the heart, the range, the depth and the magnificence of the sound that with such a lightness of touch transports and transforms you completely. Music beyond my intelligence and all that my awestruck heart wishes to hear.'

For a moment no one dared to breathe. The magic four froze, looked awkward and stared for a moment at inanimate objects. Then Fred gave a long, defeated exhale, while Nathan looked directly at Horatio and said,

'The greatest magician of our time does not wonder.

Raffaello did not wonder. He knew. There is only certainty for that unfortunate soul.'

Again the quiet in the room resonated too loudly and this time Horatio walked softly, calmly, from the room. The door closed. Gradually everyone except Nathan made polite excuses and left quickly. The door closed again. He sat alone. He looked at the discarded empty chairs, felt their vibrant blue glare and the silence more acutely. He slowly closed his eyes, believing it was all over, but hoping that it was not.

After a few moments he drew something from his pocket. It was a dream sphere that he had created in desperation and hope. He held it before him, with his elbows placed on the table and rolled it between his hands. It was cool to the touch. Created out of love and his dreams of love, it was completely from his heart, from all the times he would daydream about Esther. He looked into it then wrapped both palms around it and rested his forehead on his fingers, supporting the weight of his head as his temples throbbed. He hoped with all his heart that love could conquer all.

NATHAN LONGED for love and believed in its purity and power. Horatio longed for power and had the ruthlessness to attain it by whatever means necessary. Casting himself under an invisibility spell, Horatio followed Nathan. He observed Nathan's nervousness, as he strode purposefully behind him, unseen and unheard. And so the wolf followed its prey around the castle, knowing that whichever path it took would lead to its eventual downfall.

They came to Esther's room. Nathan vaguely observed that there was a magic presence somewhere in the corridor and looked down it. He saw nothing to alarm him. Horatio stood next to him, invisible, watching and waiting. Nathan's mind was fraught, focused on what he was about to do, his confidence wavering slightly and he was not concerned about the magic presence. It was so light, so easy to dismiss as a ghost or some remnant of minor magic at the far end of the corridor. Nathan did not imagine it was a threat. He had no idea of how deep Horatio's hatred for him ran, of how such a spell had taken months in construction to feel so waif-like and inconsequential, of how Horatio only created such things when he felt threatened and stored them for emergencies, when deception might be required.

Nathan did not realise that the man who now wanted to destroy him was standing silently by his side, as he turned the handle on Esther's door. The door was unlocked. Nathan looked around cautiously, to check he was unobserved, and then entered the room, Horatio followed. The room was bright with sunlight and colourful in décor: of birds, flowers and botanical prints. On a table by the door was a turquoise vase filled with pink moss roses that emitted a gentle perfume. Nathan took the dream sphere from his jacket pocket, looked at it for a few moments and sighed, closed his eyes, as if in silent prayer. Then he opened his eyes and threw the sphere gently into the air. It flew up above Esther's bed and stayed there, translucent and hardly visible, timed to coincide with her slumber. Then Nathan left the room.

Horatio waited until Nathan's footsteps became distant, then he materialised, clicked his fingers sharply and opened his hand. The sphere above the bed fell into his waiting palm. It swirled with images of flowers, fields and countryside. He lay on Esther's bed and skimmed through it. The images ran like poetry, but Horatio's soul was not soothed.

It was a proposal of marriage, showing Nathan's devotion, how he understood Esther's hopes and fears, how he would support her and enable her to fly to greater things than she could imagine. With references subtle and sublime to all she held dear, some so subtle that Horatio could not perceive their relevance, but he did not doubt their authenticity. His eyes were opened to the insight Nathan had into the mind of Esther and more alarmingly, the depth of Nathan's feelings, which released strange boiling sensations within Horatio.

At the end, he sat up, on the edge of her bed, composed himself and made one simple change to the dream sequence. He replaced all the images of Nathan with images of himself. In the blink of an eye he robbed Nathan's proudest magical creation of its truth. He looked into the sphere at the final scene, now of him and Esther together. He paused, tapped the sphere quickly with one finger to nudge the image of him closer to the centre then sent it flying back to where he had found it. He left the room with a sense of irritation.

Horatio did not believe that love could conquer all, but that he could conquer love. When Nathan arrived at the castle the next morning Horatio greeted him with the usual exuberant and amiable courtesy that he would offer to any guest. Fred and Violet looked at each other in relief. The four of them stood talking in the courtyard in the early morning light, when Esther Valencia burst in with the widest smile, sparkling eyes and a joy so infectious and strong, that all were uplifted in anticipation of what she would say, as she announced to the world that she would soon become Esther Drake. Nathan stood open-mouthed staring at her in disbelief. His heart had been lifted higher than he could imagine and then it had plummeted from that great height; like an executioner's sword, the words cut through his entire being, to fall at his feet, the place at which he now stared. He turned slowly and walked out of the castle.

*A*s a wedding gift for Horatio, Esther painted three scenes from the dream sphere in which he had proposed to her. They looked exactly as she had seen them. Pictures of them together, infused with love. She chose one of the past, one of the present and one of the future.

On receiving the paintings Horatio looked shocked and then tired. She stared at him in wide-eyed confusion. He quickly composed himself and followed up his reaction with his most welcoming smile and grateful platitudes. Too late, she thought, swallowing her hurt. Even his thankfulness had an agitated edge she observed. Later the same week she encountered the same tone, as he charmingly thanked some guests when she knew he could not wait for them to leave. His irritation almost spilled over, perhaps not perceptibly to them, but clearly to her.

Six months later the paintings stood in the corner of his office, on the floor, facing the wall. She hung them above his desk around the window that overlooked the courtyard, so that he could see them when he worked.

'No! Your beauty is too distracting!' he said.

He moved them to the wall behind him.

Esther never painted again.

Years later Annie saw them and adored them, so he gave them to her and she hung them in her bedroom. She showed Esther, beaming, revelling in the love of her parents and the amazing art her mother had created. Esther hugged her and tried her best to smile.

PART III

One year after the burn out of Raffaello Riviera

THE DRAGON

*T*he Firebrand roared and raced across the sky as the woman jumped down from the boat. Holding a blanket close to her chest, she walked towards the shore. The Firebrand landed on the sand before her. It stood glowering, mouth opening wide, with its face of fire tense and twisted. It gave a battle cry roar as acid and anger raged inside its stomach. Flames danced along the water's edge, as the air filled with parched smoke and the crackle of branches burning on the shoreline.

It had devoured many people from the Winter Storm who through folly or desperation had tried to return, but never had one stood so boldly before it. The Firebrand was programmed to destroy and beyond this, no conscious thought entered its mind. It hunched down on its back legs, ready to propel forward, face contorted like a silent scream, yet still she appeared unafraid.

Claudia Savine looked up at the Firebrand, forced to shield her ice-blue eyes from the light it was generating, but staring back with her own fury. The Firebrand started to speed towards her and she held up the newborn child, whose eyes should have been a chilling blue, but were as warm and welcoming as dark chocolate. Eyes that looked just like those of its creator, Raffaello Riviera. The Firebrand looked into them. It stopped and then circled in confusion; its eyes wide, brow furrowed and jaws closed.

'This is Millicent Savine, Raffaello's daughter,' Claudia shouted.

In those brown eyes the Firebrand, the burn out spell of Raffaello, encountered a problem. It was born of Raffaello's hatred, which was now reflected back through a baby's eyes, born of Raffaello's love. Those eyes momentarily cancelled out the rage. It flew to sit on the sand, looking dazed and coughing violently as it began to malfunction. The ground beneath it turned to glass and sand blasted out in all directions, stinging Claudia's arms as she protected Millicent.

To destroy the child would mean destroying something of itself. From the connections now misfiring within the spell arose the Firebrand's first independent thoughts and feelings. Fear pushed its way to the front, sharp and awakening. It grew steadily alongside the dragon's awareness of its power, its thought. The feeling and the thought spun quickly together and plunged the Firebrand into extreme anxiety, then terror. Shaking, it blew warm air, to softly place the woman and child back in the boat. Then with firmer controlled breath, to send them back to the Winter Storm. It shook violently. For the first time its urge to fight, was replaced with the urge for flight and it shot up suddenly, high into the sky, spluttering soot and black smoke. From then on it sought to exist in the most remote parts of the island, away from the eyes of the world.

Malfunctioning meant the Firebrand could never achieve internal peace. Never had the sea witches been so unpleasantly disturbed from their sleep and never had anyone seen so much steam, as the day it tried to drown itself in the sea.

Even when the poor creature weighted itself down in iron to sink, it eventually resurfaced with fizzing force, hurtled through the air, bounced in steaming hot bubbles and flew away in frustration. A hot tub sea was a peculiar and effervescent experience, which the sea witches grew to appreciate. In its regular dives to the bottom they learned the correct distance at which they should wait to ensure the most pleasing water temperature and the best place to collect the seared shrimp that would fall from its scales. Soon whole groups were waiting to greet it with lavender bath salts and pots of chilli and lime mayonnaise.

NIGHT MUSIC

Two Years after Nathan Glass walked out of Stonerock Castle

eartbreak transformed Nathan's heart and he felt it physically changing; he lived reclusively in the southern forest for two years wishing that this was not so. At night, in the forest when it rained, he would dream of black ink slowly dripping and wake in alarm. He focused on his experiments, he had many ideas; some that he had held on to from years ago, that he had wanted to develop all his life. But now things were different. His ideas started as quests for good, but no sooner than the work began, he would suddenly see how it could also be used for wicked means. The dark thought would then grow, choke the good and be all that he could think about. The drive for destruction upturned everything, ransacking his mind, pushing forward all the time. So he stopped his magic experiments. Then he sank slowly into sadness. He would sink into the mud, the decomposing leaves and the overgrown areas. He would lay motionless for hours wishing he could dissolve. He became paint-slicked with wet earth, adorned and encrusted with nature's discarded remnants.

So consumed by his misery, so inwardly focused, so unaware of night, of hailstones and falling branches was he, that the music washed over him many times before he heard it. Then one night, sat in the tallest tree with his back resting against its ancient trunk, the notes found a way in. One by one they penetrated the tight knot of his agony and he heard them for the first time.

The sound felt like cool raindrops on his face. The music was coming from high above him and he thought it must be the music of the stars. It began as a soft haunting melody with a purity of sound and within that something that resonated deep within Nathan, sadness. It was a song of sorrow to match his feelings, but lift them slightly somehow, enough to make him look up and observe the sky.

He could see a flickering star or what he thought might be a comet, but his thoughts and gaze did not linger. He curled himself into a ball, listening to the music, feeling it build and fade out. Then he closed his eyes and returned to drowning out the world, entrenched in the pain of self-pity.

Since he had left the castle, he existed in the forest: climbing, wandering and only eating when his hunger drummed so loudly in his stomach that food was needed to silence it. He felt little other than the weight of hopelessness until the music returned and lifted him out, just enough to remind him that he was still alive: sad and sorry for himself, battered and broken, but still here, right now in this tree, looking up to where the music came from and seeing again something that looked like a comet.

This pattern continued for many months. Each time the music arrived a small sense of comfort began to build inside Nathan, growing with each visit. He listened more intently.

He swayed in time to the rhythm and mouthed the words at first, then began to whisper them and eventually he sang. He kept singing until he reached the top of his voice, so loud and strong that each low note would slide down the tree deep into the earth and each high note rise up to the heavens. Soon the longing for the music merged and interwove with his sorrow and he craved it until its return, when he would sit up straight and let the music soothe his soul.

As the relief and contentment inside him grew, his eyes focused on the comet with greater clarity, all those miles away. He began to wonder if it was a comet at all. There was an undulating spiral that shone brightly like a tail of golden dust. Usually when the music began to fade he would close his eyes to listen and savour its final moments. Once, just as he was about to close his eyes, he looked a second longer at the strange illumination in the sky and saw what he had missed in all his months of being enchanted by the music. He realised that the moving light was not the tail of a comet at all, but what looked like the tail of a restless fire dragon.

The dragon was at a distance, yet much closer than the stars. Nathan kept his attention on its light and saw far, far away the creature uncurl and fly with powerful wings across the sky. He recognised its shape. He gasped and almost smiled. The Firebrand. He watched Raffaello's dragon, observed some tentative movements and knew that its magic was faulting.

The heaviness that had weighed Nathan down began to shift. Inside his body, it felt as if large marble pebbles were falling, click-clacking, moving around and dissipating. His eyes were open and his curiosity awoke. His fears for his sanity floated unnoticed away. The lasting legacy of Raffaello Riviera was burning in the sky above him, a miserable creature whose pain he understood. As dawn broke and the last marble stone fell he experienced an amazing sense of clarity.

The new Scion must be able to tame the creation of the previous greatest magician and that task, that purpose, he decided, was now his. The weight inside and around him had gone. He was ignited.

With an unfamiliar and heady sense of excitement he stood up and he ran, bare-feet slipping as he did so. He ran and ran until he saw his path was about to be blocked by the cool rushing river that meandered through the forest. He saw it and sped up. He ran and jumped, launching himself recklessly, crashing heavily into its depths, rocketing boldly, turning in its currents, splashing, gasping deeply for breath and feeling euphorically alive. Then he floated, letting the current take him, immersing the back of his head into the cold water, his hair spreading, anemone-like as he began to plan.

Vast distances had to be covered. So he ran up the sky. With time and patience he could have perfected flying or come up with something more elegant, but right then he had neither. So his strong legs ran barefoot up into the inky blue night to the first viewing platform he had created, an illusion of wood that looked like a raft you might swim out to at sea. This was the first stopping point, a wait-and-see point. He did not want to come too close, too soon. He needed to protect himself from the fire and he wanted the dragon's trust.

Not knowing when the dragon would appear, he got used to running up the sky most evenings. His legs were shocked by such intense activity and he gasped for breath each time. He would puff and wheeze at the top of the platform. The aching muscles the next day served as a sharp biting reminder of what he was trying to do. What he was going to do.

When his breath came more easily, when the route up the sky was a familiar and integrated part of his evening and when he felt completely at ease and alert as he waited on the platform, the Firebrand flew in. It curled up in its usual place directly above the tallest tree in the southern forest and rested, miles and miles away in the sky. It began its song softly and Nathan basked in the relief it brought him as he watched the gently undulating tail. If the Firebrand saw him it took no notice.

Nathan adored the intricacy of the Firebrand's design: the contrasting colours of flames that would appear in tiny flickers when it moved, the beauty in the menacing face with its strong features that were both terrifying and yet wondrous. He knew he was seeing exactly what Raffaello Riviera had seen in his imagination and it was the most glorious manifestation of magic he had ever seen.

Seven visits and seven new platforms later, each allowing him to edge a little closer, Nathan finally piqued the curiosity of the dragon. He looked up and the dragon looked down into his eyes, still from a distance. Immediately the dragon's tail started to beat. Restlessly it prepared to flee, in fear of accidentally cremating the man. But then it noticed that the man's clothes were not drenched in perspiration and he was not shielding his eyes from the strong light. The dragon paused. The man was perfectly calm, looking up and smiling. The dragon gave a long slow blink as if to prove its eyes were not deceiving it. Nathan waved and the dragon watched, then closed its eyes, made itself comfortable and commenced its song.

The next time the dragon came, it saw Nathan before it found its usual spot. It slowed its flight, the usual glide replaced by a hesitant beating of wings. It settled itself, but kept one eye open, watching Nathan, flicking its tail in agitation. Nathan waved. The Firebrand opened both eyes together and the muscles of its face creased up around them.

Nathan noted its discomfort and held tightly to the raft, trying to keep calm. The dragon let out a long slow breath that shot flames and bright sparks in Nathan's direction. Nathan rubbed his hands together, then turned his palms towards the dragon as if to warm them and smiled. The dragon's tail beat faster and its lungs filled like bellows as it inhaled. It held its breath and saw to its amazement that the man was sitting down, his legs dangling over the edge of the platform, holding two ice creams, eating one and offering the other up to the Firebrand. The dragon breathed out. The raft and Nathan were engulfed in flames for a few seconds, but completely unaffected and unmoved, the ice creams still solid.

The dragon closed its eyes and began its song. Nathan joined in. The dragon stopped. Nathan stopped. The dragon began again. Nathan began again. The dragon stopped, Nathan continued, pitch perfect. The dragon hunched up, looking for a moment as if it might lunge towards Nathan, then relaxed and joined in the song, louder than ever before. Nathan's eyes sparkled. When the dragon came to the end of its song Nathan clapped and the dragon began the song all over again. Nathan laughed then joined in. When the song came to a close again, Nathan waited. The dragon's eyes opened wide and its brow furrowed in concentration. It looked focused and dangerous. It leaped forward and flew at speed towards Nathan, who sat frozen, a fixed smile on his face, the taste of vanilla cloying in his dry mouth. The dragon's jaws opened wide. Nathan saw the raging face of fire coming towards him, the red flames of its open mouth and throat. He closed his eyes. The jaws snapped together at his hand. When he dared to open them the dragon was making its way across the sky and the second ice cream had gone. Nathan lay back on the platform in contentment, watching his soon-to-be companion making its elegant retreat towards the stars, golden and magnificent against the night sky.

The next morning, in the early hours, Nathan created the darkness. His magic, which had remained almost dormant in his misery, was now wide awake and spinning uncontrollably through every cell of his body. Driven by his desire to escape the world, but now to help the dragon too, he wanted a home, a place to hide, a safe place for him and the dragon to be broken and free. The evocative music of the Firebrand played in his mind as he worked. He built his vision, pushing forward with his hands; making open, sweeping gestures with his arms as glittering black clouds of smoke arose all around him. The foundations, the building blocks were opaque black shapes with volatile movement. They soared upward and turned sharply, twinkling and metallic as they reflected the light and revealed the architectural structures within. As his creation grew the shapes loomed like angular dark spectres surrounding him.

Within the darkness he created many rooms including the flame room, where the dragon could exist in comfort, with cool winds and relief from its troubled state. The Firebrand's light, that could blind and blister was dimmed to the glow of a welcoming log fire and its size reduced to that of a large hound, actions it could reverse should it wish to, but it did not. Nathan's black heart with its white speck adored the decision to entice the Firebrand into the darkness, for the Firebrand was as powerful as the once greatest magician and could be programmed to destroy. Its mind and muscles constantly resisted the destruction it was programmed for, which meant it grew stronger every day.

THE SAVINES

*F*orty-five years after the Firebrand had looked into Millicent Savine's brown eyes she returned to the island. This time as a grown woman with her own teenage daughter Fifer and the dragon instinctively sensed their arrival. It awoke with Raffaello's rage rekindled, hate, pain and sorrow all crackling in the pyre. It saw flashes of them in its mind, enough to discern their location and it fled its calm dark sanctuary at speed, intent on finding its prey. The Firebrand circled in the sky above them and looked into their brown eyes. They were the direct descendants of Raffaello. It watched them, crippled with indecision, and let them walk along the beach unhindered, then fled back to the darkness. Claudia Savine never returned; she believed she had only that one chance to gain freedom for her daughter and would be lucky to escape again with her own life. The Firebrand, having thought about it for some time, felt the same.

MILLICENT WENT to the Blacksmith's shop, which was weathered and crumbling, untouched since the evening Raffaello had summoned the Winter Storm. It belonged to the Savine family and she was going to make it a home for herself and Fifer. The children of Escaville watched the tall woman with long dark hair open the door that they always believed could never be opened. From a distance they stared through the cobwebbed windows as Millicent set to work with the broom. Spiders scuttled out and other creatures that had found peace and quiet in the unused shop made their hasty exits. As she swept, other things began to happen inside: the windows cleared, metal objects leapt like frogs from the floor on to the workbench, trailing dust, grime and detritus, which hung from them like matted hair. On the workbench, the items set themselves upright and the dirt coating them began to disappear. The children played a guessing game to work out what each item was as it gradually restored before their eyes.

'A cat! A pot! No, it's a kettle!'

Fifer, who had lingered outside watching their reactions, set to work on the exterior. The broken sign on the ground, next to the children, flew up like a startled bird. They all jumped, squealed with excitement and watched open-mouthed as it reattached itself to its post. Its cracked yellow paint smoothed like butter, the vibrant colour slowly returning, glowing against the bold ebony lettering of Savine. Fifer smiled, her eyes bright as the word stood out, like an announcement to the world. Next the metal doorplate, which was a leaden, dull brown with flecks of green, the colours of a damp winter garden, began to brighten. As if the sun was glowing behind it, the metal lit up and burned away the tarnish to show the brightness of the original brass. Proudly polished it revealed the swirls of an engraved letter S and the reflections of the children's faces.

Millicent started up the furnace. The heat, rumble and

smell of burning dust rose up and out of the now open windows. From then on the children called Millicent the Fire Witch and would dare each other to touch the newly polished handle of the Blacksmith's shop. They imagined that the fire in the forge was hotter than the sun and was full of creatures that wanted to eat their souls. Millicent was delighted when her first customer told her this and hung a broom with elaborate, gothic ironwork in the window. She would widen her eyes and stare pointedly at any little faces that dared to peep over the sill.

The young men of Escaville called Millicent a witch when, without magic, she won the Cavanagans arm-wrestling competition, hands down. Her long sinewy fore-arms easily overpowered the sweaty palms of her grunting, teeth-grinding, pink-faced opponents. It was a psychological game that she enjoyed: for the steel in her mind was harder and stronger than bone or muscle. Amused by her nickname, she wore her hair long and took to only wearing black, which was practical for working in the smithy, made the laundry a much less fussy affair and gave her more time for her magic.

As a teenager, growing up in the Winter Storm, Millicent used to ask her magic friends to show her their latest tricks, discoveries or experiments. She would observe them and their magic closely. Andreas might try to turn into a snow leopard, Jemima to create a telescope out of ice and Clayton to make the penguins perform in a string quartet. She would work out not only how their magic worked, but also the exact way in which their minds performed it, so she could block it. After enjoying their results, she would ask them to perform it again. Each of them would try and not be able to. She was reversing their magic before it could fully begin. Her satisfaction grew alongside their annoyance as they stamped and cursed. Millicent would eventually walk away whistling a happy tune. She trained like an Olympian to be better and faster and soon her favourite question was 'Could you show me that again?' After about six months, every magician in the Winter Storm was well and truly fed up with her.

On some days she would stop them all before they started. Surreptitiously, she blocked in increasing numbers the magicians of the Winter Storm. She watched, she learned, she conquered. After a year of focused concentration and quiet observation came the day she had planned for. On the day that they were blown into in a new territory, she stopped them all, those who were older and wiser and those who were younger and fresher. No magic today. It did not take them long to realise their magic could not be activated in this new land to which the storm had brought them. Panic set in. A meeting was called. Claudia Savine met with the Falstaffs and the other magic families. They could not understand what had happened, everyone looked concerned, everyone was talking, how would they keep warm? All except Millicent who sat on a rock, scanning for polar bears, whistling softly, unperturbed.

Claudia walked up to her and glared. Millicent did not look at her, but said

'I want the feathers from the cape petrel, that Andreas Falstaff found and put in his hat. So beautiful. I want to wear them in my hair,' she smiled as she turned to face her mother.

Two days later the feathers were forcefully removed from Andreas's hat by his father and given to Claudia, who found Millicent sitting on her ice rock scanning the vast expanse of white with keen eyes. Millicent fixed them in her hair. All was well and their magic returned immediately. As soon as it did, her mother sent her a shooting glance, which sent her flying backwards, off the rock and into a puddle of iced water. Millicent shrieked in surprise, although perhaps she should have not been so surprised. Claudia walked away feeling an uncomfortable mix of indignation and pride.

FIFER SAVINE WAS BORN on the same day as Aldemus Drake, their births less than an hour apart. Both Esther Drake and Millicent Savine had contracted and watered, bounced and cursed their way through long arduous days, sweat-faced and beautiful, cheeks rosy as apples, before the arrival of their purple screaming joy, their first child. Esther gave birth in a castle, where the sounds echoed down the stone walls and around corners; Millicent in an ice cave on a bear skin rug, her hot feet and hands melting everything she touched.

Fifer Savine had a sweet face, with large feline eyes and petite stature that belied the hardness inside and the history of her early years. Millicent loved her daughter with as much warmth as her thawing heart could give, aware that she was herself a woman broken by ice and eternal winter. When the two of them came to the island and felt its warmth it made them uncomfortable and uncertain, but they grew more accepting and appreciative of it with every year that passed.

Fifer Savine was ambitious in every way; fuelled by desire that comes from deprivation. The things she wanted were things that she never had or had in such scarcity that the taste of their meagre crumbs was as close to torture as pleasure. She wanted everything that had been beyond the reach of her family before her. Freedom, which she now had and recognition for the Savine line of magic, which was the battle she fought for everyday, but hidden to her and stronger still, the invisible ogre that she desired most was love.

Fifer Savine was far too good at magic to keep her mother reassured that life would be easy and uneventful. Millicent gave her independence. Fifer wandered through the southern forest, even when night's shadows raced in thick and fast as charging cavalry. In the dark forest her fear and excitement ran hand in hand.

As the years went by Fifer could still clearly remember the face of her grandmother, Claudia Savine, with her fierce blue eyes and welcoming smile, but gradually her childhood in the Winter Storm began to fade from her mind. When she tried to remember, she could feel the immobilising cold and hear the shriek of arctic birds echoing across vast white space, but the details dissolved. When she asked her mother how she, Millicent, used her magic, Millicent told her,

'I personally have only ever used my magic for the greater good. You must do the same. Talent grows from hard work, perseverance and deep respect for your elders of magic lineage.'

Fifer would venture into the edges of the southern forest with her friends, two puppyish boys who adored her and a girl who was sometimes motherly towards her. It was frightening and fun when night came and they stayed out there in the dark. They would run and hide and make the noises of owls, wolves and forest creatures, then jump out and terrify each other, before laughing and coming together again in relief.

One evening, just as they came together after adrenalin fuelled forest games, something charged at them from the night-dark undergrowth. It was an angry wild boar. It knocked her motherly friend into the mud and startled the boys who ran away in hurried panic. The boar was fast and strong. It charged at Fifer. She dodged too late. Her body escaped, but as her arm moved to balance her, her hand caught and tore on its tusk. It showered blood. She did not scream. The boar halted mid-charge. She had stopped the creature. It stilled, panting, its eyes fixed ahead, stunned. She had worked so quickly in her mind to stop him, she was not sure what she had done, but all of the magic she knew was activated. He was frozen, transfixed, diverted from his purpose. That moment stayed with her, standing in the semi-darkness, chest thumping, cold air against her face, the smell of damp earth, her hand wet, electric-stinging, the creature and her both frightened, breathless, watching each other. The boar calmed to steady breathing.

'Leave now,' Fifer whispered.

It turned its heavy frame and trundled deep into the trees. Her friend groaned and stumbled towards her. They used the sleeve of Fifer's cardigan to bandage her hand.

It was late when Fifer arrived home, but her mother was still up working. Millicent said nothing, yet looked pointedly at Fifer's bandaged hand, which was soaked through with blood.

'It's nothing, I cut myself on some brambles,' Fifer said.

Millicent looked at the hand and then at Fifer, who felt the sharp pinch and yelped as stitches wove beneath the dressing. Her mother went back to her work without speaking and Fifer went to bed.

On another such evening in the forest Fifer fell into an ancient swampy hole. Its crumbling leaf and moss surface had blended with the forest floor. She fell two metres down and hit viscous water, from which she could not extricate herself. She panicked trying to tread water. Her magic seemed to fail her as she attempted to escape. The motherly friend and the puppy faced boys tried to help, but soon got bored. They left her and did not return. They did not get help. She floundered for hours. She heard wild animals stalking through the brushwood above. Eventually, dazed and exhausted, as she drifted in and out of consciousness, she slowly directed the nearest tree roots through the soil towards her. They pushed though the mud, rupturing the ground around her. She grabbed them, climbed up and hauled herself out. She berated herself as she walked home cold and shivering, for not seeing the patterns to free herself sooner. Fear, then sadness had taken over. She would snuff that out. That would not happen again.

And then alone in the forest, a few years later, when she was nineteen, waiting for dusk, before heading home, she saw a strange flickering in the sky. The forest became as black as night before night had fully fallen. The change alarmed her. She was on the edge of a clearing and was suddenly aware of movement in the forest and of muffled sound. She could feel the presence of other people, hidden. As the black clouds descended she heard footsteps of people running, from different directions, towards the flickering black. Lanterns and torches were suddenly lit, carried by the watchers. The illuminated faces appeared of magicians she recognised heading towards the blackness, people who drank at the pub that looked like a church. Then she knew that this was the darkness that she had heard them talk of; the burn out spell of a man called Nathan Glass. Magic lay inside the place he had created; power that they ravenously coveted.

Close to her, a woman of solid build ran past wearing a bonnet adorned with charcoal roses, more rose than it was hat. Then came a ferocious man, huge as a buffalo; then a man in a military hat, whose speed surprised her from his gnarled face and twisted posture, as he zipped into the clearing. More people appeared around the edges, waited momentarily, then sprinted and disappeared into the darkness beneath the strange glimmer above. Her instincts told her that these were not good magicians. Fifer stood perfectly still, shocked and afraid. Reeling from what she was seeing, her amazement grew. Look what at what the night can hold, hidden and unexpected, she thought. Then slowly, somewhere beyond the terror, a smile began to appear and thoughts of exhilaration grew.

THE FIGMENTS

*I*n the darkness Betty tucked her smooth grey hair behind her ears, looked up from her desk with interest and smiled at the visitor.

'I'm Betty. I am one of those, what do you call it? Figments. From his imagination.'

The visitor's eyes opened wide in surprise. Betty gave a kind smile, the one she used to make people feel at ease.

'Aye, I'm not real, although it feels like I am, but no. I think creating me helped him feel safe. So, anyway, when he cuts off from the game, stops creating rooms and talking to the visitors, he goes into the contemplation room and that's it. Won't come out for ages, can go months at a time. It's his bad heart you see. Sets him off. Not nice. Looks nice in there though,' Betty said, indicating to a door nearby. 'I've had glimpses of a huge canyon, wild landscape. Nathan sits on the rock and stares at the river deep below or into the distance, which stretches for miles, all green and beautiful. A door to another world, except none of it is real, just in his head. And then out of his head to create the room. Magic's wonderful, fascinating. I'd have me a beach though and something softer to sit on. '

'I'd like to meet him.'

'Everyone wants to meet him. Every single one of the mad carnival that pass through this place. And yet he's such a lonely boy, always a lonely boy. Your name?'

The visitor paused and whispered a reply. Betty slid a brown leather book across the desk and opened it cautiously, then officiously looked the visitor up and down.

'Really? No one's ever been allowed in that room. Just him, until now.'

'Until now?'

'Yes,' Betty smiled. 'You're on the list. He thought you would come. You're one of his predictions, his latest preoccupation. You can go through.'

Betty put a tick next to the name, which was at the top of a short list of names, the rest of which the visitor tried to read, but Betty quickly closed the book.

'That's the door, go in. When you find him, ask if he wants a cup of tea.'

THE FIGMENTS of Nathan Glass's imagination, drawn out from the twisted recesses of his mind, have been transformed into people within the darkness. They work for him and are the hosts of the different rooms. So well formed are they that they sometimes believe they are real, or more accurately they choose to forget that they are unreal, a denial of their non-existence. Despite their posturing and competing for his attention, his illusions are a functional team bound by the tentacles of his emotions.

If someone enters the darkness whom Nathan decides he likes, the figments will in turn welcome the new arrival, although some more reluctantly than others. If Nathan is unsure of someone, the figments' behaviour will alter in line with his doubts. If someone enters the darkness that he immediately dislikes, he or she will last only a matter of moments. A firm hand, usually Katy Cavelle's as she is the most protective figment, shoves him or her out onto the highway.

What really makes the figments dance and earn their gold lettered room signs, is when someone enters the darkness whom Nathan fears. Nathan will always want that visitor to stay, despite the uncomfortable feelings they cause, because he will want to overcome his fear, even at the risk of being destroyed, should that person turn out to be the rising Scion and the Scion not be him. When Nathan feels fear the figments have to deal with their own internal panic, which manifests deeply and differently in all of them.

'NATHAN MAY WELL BE the Scion, but there is always room for doubt,' Katy Cavelle once said earnestly, her bright-green eyes alert with focus.

'There is no room for doubt! He must be the Scion. As there *is* no room for doubt!' Betty repeated and laughed loudly.

Katy looked at Betty, first with uncertainty, then with withering reproach. Katy's mouth was open, but she was speechless and nothing found its way out.

'Room! Get it? Or he would have created it! A doubt room! It'd be all grey and smoky with nowhere to sit comfortably, a small narrow room, with a secret doorway to a certainty room!' Betty was enjoying herself now. A quiet sigh of distain fell from Katy's lips, like the unwanted bite of a maggoted-apple. With a swish of her razor sharp bob she walked away as Betty continued to chuckle.

PART IV

The year Annabelle Drake wrote the History of Stonerock Castle

THE DRAKE CHILDREN

*L*ouisa joined Aldemus at the breakfast table and placed a beautiful red, leather book down next to her.

'What's that?' he asked. He picked it up and opened it. It was filled with her handwriting in midnight ink.

'I want to record and classify the magic of our guests.'

Aldemus grinned, as if he found this amusing. This irritated her, but she continued,

'Real and minor magic are easy enough to distinguish, although I do not like those terms, but I would really like to classify real magic by its skill level…'

'Morning!' said Annabelle loudly, bounding into the room. Her white-blonde curls had risen with bed-static to a significant height. Aldemus was momentarily distracted and then entertained by her appearance. Annie's hair made her look like a beautiful mixture of angel baby and wild sculptress. 'Ooh pretty book, is it full of stories?' asked Annie.

'Louisa is setting up a system. She wants to use it to record the magic of our guests,' said Aldemus. Annie laughed.

'Louisa, you are so funny,' she said.

'I'm going to do it. It will help us understand who can do what and perhaps we can then decide who should mix with who,' Louisa replied.

Aldemus's eyebrows came together in concern.

'You want to tell people who they should speak to?' he asked.

'No. I want to find the most talented and allow them to learn from one another,' Louisa replied.

Aldemus buttered a crumpet aggressively.

'Our guests do not come here to be measured with tape measures. Stonerock is a place where people are treated as equals; even the weakest magician has talent that can be appreciated,' he said.

'Musically talented minor magic!' said Annie with pride then added with a smile, 'You can just put me in as a footnote if you like.'

Louisa sighed.

'It was more to categorise real magic into first order, second order and third order…'

Aldemus banged his fist on the table, looked at Annie and said in a mock-stern voice,

'Not for the likes of you young lady, minor magic can only mix with swine!' Aldemus and Annie laughed. Louisa drank her coffee quickly and left the table.

Louisa and Aldemus Drake were both real magic and very talented. Louisa had a very organised mind; everything in neatly labelled boxes, with nothing loose or able to wriggle free. Aldemus had a mind that constantly wriggled free. In his there were no boxes, everything whizzed around at incredible speed, like a thrilling fairground ride, controlled and fast. Annie was minor magic, but her mind worked in a similar way to Aldemus's at a pace that was more relaxed, more like a ride on a carousel with pleasing music.

Louisa began labelling the castle guests in her book, without telling them what she was doing, as she knew that would infuriate her brother. She listened carefully to their conversations, watched their experiments and asked specific questions of each one. She would then put ticks and crosses in her book against their magical abilities, which she would define in great detail. She devised cunning methods to see who excelled at different things, a game to see who could perform a spell in the quickest time or with the most precision. Who could get a howler monkey to make the loudest sound? She had started with loud creatures in general, but Frederick Cavanagan would always appear at just the wrong moment and win with a Tiger pistol shrimp.

The competitive instincts of the magic four were obstacles Louisa had to meander around to get the best from some of the other guests. So she would often start an activity with all four of them together and then disappear off to do the real work. Who could dissolve the room or disappear? Imitate fire? Transform into a cicada? The magicians enjoyed the competition and attention, loved to talk about themselves and thought that Louisa was wonderful fun. They did not dream that she was testing them. She encouraged them to play magical games for hours, then at the end of the day would go to her room and spend all evening writing detailed notes about each one.

THE SKY WAS BRIGHT BLUE; the beach somewhat desolate and the sea air had a biting chill, which allowed Aldemus to wear his new coat that he was exceedingly pleased with. It was red with gold embellishments and black military lines. It made him feel commanding and want to stamp his boots together in attention at the same time. He helped some of the elderly gentlemen who were making their way precariously across the rocks, holding his balance when they were losing theirs. When everyone was in position he began the lesson.

'I've emptied the rock pools of life, so if each of you could kindly stand by one, we can begin. I've marked them with driftwood crosses,' said Aldemus.

'Here Aldemus?' asked one of the lovely ladies in the front row, who were never late, always eager and occasionally swooned, well one or two of them anyway, much to his satisfaction. Aldemus was hoping for a beautiful collection in the front row by the end of the year. He enjoyed teaching magic.

'Yes, perfect. Get comfortable. Try to clear your mind of all distractions. I want you all to focus on the water in your rock pool. Look deep into it, concentrate. Later we will try and imagine life in there, conjure images in our imagination and see what we can do with them, but for now just look.'

He liked pure obedience when he gave his instruction. The ladies of the front row immediately complied. An elderly gentleman, concentrating on the ladies in the front row, was slower. Some were distracted by the cold wind and fiddled with fastenings and outer garments. To his annoyance a young boy at the back was stirring the rock pool with his finger.

'Am I too late?' asked a voice. Yes! Thought Aldemus in irritation, before he looked up. Fifer Savine was running, perfectly balanced, down a treacherous rock slope, her short brown hair was windswept and her smile was wide. The class watched her confident descent in surprise.

'There is space at the back. You're lucky,' he snapped.

She smiled and saluted, 'Nice coat captain!'

Aldemus looked up through lowered eyes. Then smiled despite himself.

'Concentrate on the rock pool.'

. . .

ALDEMUS DRAKE WAS solid and tall with dark hair and eyes, his father's son, yet with a quick mobility, sharper and more graceful than Horatio. Horatio was a stomper, Aldemus light on his feet, although you would not expect it from his stature.

'Built for ballroom dancing,' Violet would always say of Aldemus as she watched him shift from languid repose into an effortless acrobatic movement. He spent much time in repose, like a cat in the sun, to his mother Esther's annoyance. Aldemus had a sharp magic mind that nature had proudly presented, but coupled with an inclination to let its embers smoulder rather than stoke the fire with vigour. Esther did not question the talent of her first born, only his ambition. He was lucky, perhaps too lucky. She sometimes thought and feared that being raised in a castle and being born of two notorious magic families allowed him to wake up every morning and think 'job done'. However, when he offered to teach magic, the tight expression that Esther so often wore when thinking of him, softened, as he knew it would. He taught most frequently away from the castle, in the forests and caves, on the lakes and shorelines, to escape her enthusiasm and kind suggestions. Horatio saw his son as the golden boy; a pleasing reminder of his own youth with a quickness of step that he liked to imagine was once his.

Louisa came next and any ambition Aldemus lacked she made up for, with a tenacity and single mindedness that delighted her mother and secretly terrified her father. Most people agreed that she would be hugely successful in whatever aspect of magic she chose to pursue. She had a serious face and her father's dark features, like Aldemus, but unlike him, the pale skin of her mother. If she spent weeks studying, with less sunlight than was probably good for her, the pallor took on its own luminescence and became almost ghostly.

Aldemus, like both his parents, was convivial and entertaining; Louisa introverted with seemingly less need for the gaieties and fripperies of life. She knew her own mind more clearly than anyone her father had ever met and seeing as he could rarely charm or impress her, Horatio was at a loss with what to do with her, of how to be around her. Although he loved her with all his heart, he would often find himself mumbling, 'Louisa, you can never please her.'

Then came Annie, the bundle of joy, bouncing golden-white curls and beaming smile. Energetic, interested in a thousand things at once, caring, kind, distracted and distracting. Horatio's energy was passion and fire, Esther's cool as polished steel, Annie, unlike her siblings did not inherit their magic force, but simple minor magic in musical fields. Her vivacity came from living life, creating magic and music in perfect harmony, it appeased and balanced the infernos and frosts brought by the rest of her family and she was easily adored. Annie was accepting of others, Louisa silently judgemental, Aldemus fickle as a three year old, depending on his desire of the hour.

FIFER SAVINE WAS NOW LETTING her beautiful brown eyes focus attentively on the rock pool in front of her.

'SHE'S ARROGANT,' said Aldemus, later to his mother.

'So you say. And have said more than once,' replied Esther, rolling dream spheres across an antique writing desk and losing count. Aldemus paced around the room.

'Why come to class if you can already create? She is more

than minor magic. She came to show off. An alligator! In a rock pool.'

'Perhaps she wants to learn. There is always more to learn and we all make mistakes.'

'It wasn't a mistake. She likes attention.'

'So do you.'

'Not like that.'

'Like what?'

'So brazenly, to distract everyone, without care, to completely disrupt the class and cause pandemonium.'

'Were people upset?'

'No. They ran around like hapless idiots.'

'Did they learn?'

Aldemus's jaw dropped then closed firmly, his brow furrowing in irritation.

'Why am I even talking to you about this?'

'Well, they are lucky they had you to put things right, restore order and show them how things should be done. You are a good teacher. Magic needs to be executed with control.'

'Yes,' said Aldemus relaxing his glare.

Esther put the spheres aside and looked up smiling.

'Is she pretty?'

Aldemus exhaled loudly and paced out of the room.

FIFER THREW her boots into the corner of the forge and stretched out like a cat before examining the latest ironwork her mother had created.

'They look like weapons,' she said.

'Maybe, but only as a secondary purpose. That one is a walking stick, those are for making lace and this to decorate a grave. I hear you've been at the castle again.'

'Yeees mother.'

'You are smiling and laughing more these days.'

Fifer gave an exaggerated grin and perched on a stool.

'Do you have friends there? A boyfriend?' asked Millicent.

'Acquaintances. I'm too focused on my magic,' she replied as she picked up a needle and tested its sharpness against her finger.

'All work and no play...'

'Would make me you mother,' said Fifer, with a smile, to soften her words.

'I go to Cavanagans,' Millicent protested, as she moved a bag of coal.

'To win bets and humiliate fools; yes, I suppose that is sport.'

'I like the music. Pass me that cane.'

'Well, I like the music at the castle,' said Fifer, handing her the cane with a grin, brown eyes sparkling, which Millicent could sense, but did not acknowledge. She took the cane and attached the ironwork. 'There was a violinist today, Lucet Sophia, the sound was so sweet and yet so sad. You should come and listen someday.'

Millicent picked up a toasting fork made of iron lattice work and shook it at her in mock annoyance. Fifer smiled.

ALDEMUS STEPPED out into the courtyard looking at a bright blue morning sky with pure white clouds, his heart filling with vitality. Then he saw her. In a red silk jumpsuit, practising an incantation with Nicholas Rumpkin. He was startled to see Fifer and surprised by her company. Nicholas Rumpkin, rarely seen around the castle, was rumoured to use dark magic and conduct cruel experiments with animals. He stood solemnly, a tall twisted figure in a military hat, in contrast to Fifer who was upright, poised and energetic. Aldemus wondered, doubtfully, if she knew about Rumpkin's reputation. He watched them for a few moments, his good feeling dampened. Rumpkin was overseeing her magic, giving direction and commands to which she willingly complied. Aldemus was about to walk back inside, when Horatio came up to him and said conspiratorially,

'That's Fifer Savine.'

'I know.'

'Need to keep an eye on the Savine line. Her mother Millicent is rather exceptional; she has developed quite a reputation.'

'A code breaker.'

'Yes. Last week she released three ancient trolls, couple of hundred years old.'

'Wow. Where from?'

'You know the towering boulders in the southern forest near the crag?'

'Yes.'

'They are boulders no more. It seems she walked past them once; thought the formation looked odd, went away, came back that evening and released them on her first attempt. Amazing. The trolls are coming to dinner tonight, Millicent declined.'

'I've heard she is not a fan.'

'Maybe. Her daughter is delightful and seems happy to be here though.' Horatio raised an eyebrow and looked at Aldemus, who shook his head softly. 'And I am so lucky to have such a charming son.' Aldemus looked at the floor, his face flushing slightly. Horatio patted him on the back and said, 'Get to work,' before striding off to greet Frederick Cavanagan.

'WHERE DO you come from Fifer Savine?' asked Aldemus.

She smiled at him.

'I live at the forge with my mother.'

'The forge that stood dilapidated for my entire childhood and which now sparkles like a shiny new pin.'

'The Savine line has been on this island for many years. As long as the Drakes I'm sure. This is where I am from,' she replied, still smiling.

'But there were no Savines for a long time.'

'Yes. That must have been hard for everyone.'

Aldemus laughed. 'But I am here now,' said Fifer.

'And those eyes, they sparkle in rich colour. They are not cold topaz. They have been tested, by magicians here, surreptitiously.'

'And not so surreptitiously. Waftey as good as poked me in the eye.'

'And they have never been blue.'

'Never.' A huge grin now.

'Where are you from Fifer Savine?'

She sighed ruefully and her smile left briefly. On the wall behind her in faint, but unmistakable stone script appeared momentarily the line, *Where the cold winds blow, in lands of fear, ice and snow.* Aldemus blinked in astonishment. The Stone-carved poetry spell had woken up. Fifer snapped out of her reverie and her eyes were alive again, alert and interested, looking at him. Puzzled by the arrival of poetry, Aldemus wondered, could this be a significant occasion? He was surprised by the spell, as he had not considered it to be one, but mused that maybe it felt like one to her? The beginning of something wonderful, to be here, in the castle with him, Aldemus Drake! This thought thrilled him and his smile matched hers in mischief and delight. He moved closer. She took his arm.

'Far, far away,' she eventually replied, her smile fading. He did not want it to fade. He wrapped his arm around her.

'You have beautiful eyes. I'm very glad you're here.'

'Thank you.'

'Let me show you around.'

ALDEMUS OPENED the large double doors to the great hall.

'This is the great hall,' he said, in the proprietary tone of his father.

They stepped into the vast room with its ancient vaulted ceiling. Silk tapestries hung from the stone walls. At one end there was a raised gallery intricately decorated with winged cherubs and gilded flowers. It had tiered seats with a clear view of the hall and the stone platform at the opposite end.

'It's amazing,' said Fifer.

'It's great. Definitely above average.'

Fifer walked around looking up and then went to each doorway within the room, touching them, feeling the grain of the wood.

'Such beautiful doors.'

'Great doors.'

'Yes, I was thinking so very, very great! Strong too.'

He gestured to some chairs by a large fireplace and they both sat.

'Where one can sit and watch the great and the grand!' Fifer exclaimed, sitting up straight and placing her hands neatly in her lap.

'And escape when they become incredibly dull,' he added.

'Grand people dull? Never! Never.'

'Precisely.'

They smiled and then looked at each other. The vast space seemed to shrink around them, so that it was only them, focused on each other. Neither was certain of what to say next and both eagerly drank in the other's features to solidify them in memory. The silence, strong and solid, contrasted with the whizzing thoughts and disconcerting feelings rushing around inside them. As the seconds elapsed the corners of Fifer's mouth began to turn up again and Aldemus felt flustered. He immediately focused on gaining control and removed himself from the smile that if it should form again might unbalance him. He stood, looked away and offered her his hand.

'And there's dancing, do not forget that.'

She stood. He took her arm and waist and they began to waltz. He could look at her now and focus his mind on his movements, determined to impress and compete.

'You're a good dancer,' Fifer said.

'Sort out the music Savine.'

She rolled her eyes and then concentrated as the sound of a piano and violin filled the room; the notes sliding in elegantly to the rhythm of their feet. He added a cello and another violin.

'Not bad for a blacksmith's daughter.'

'We can forge many things.'

Sharp footsteps entered the room and shattered their reverie. They looked up to see Louisa.

'Aldemus there you are. I was…I assumed it was Annie playing.'

'Fifer, meet my sister Louisa.'

Aldemus pulled apart from Fifer and bowed to his sister in amusement, still holding Fifer's hand. Fifer curtsied and giggled.

Louisa stood open mouthed.

'Does father know she's in here?'

'It's his wish.'

Louisa looked at Fifer.

'Oh. New *friends* have to be approved by our dear father before they are welcomed in. You must have impressed him.'

'Thank you.'

'Fifer, one of the violins is out of tune. It is not yours.

Show him what he is doing wrong with his magic and we will all be grateful.'

'Louisa,' said Aldemus in outraged disbelief, his good humour gone, 'It is not.'

'Listen, Aldemus listen to it!'

'You're wrong.'

'She's not. It is only slightly and easy to rectify,' said Fifer and squeezed his hand encouragingly.

Aldemus closed his eyes, hung his head and shook it muttering, 'Louisa, Louisa, Louisa.'

Louisa nodded respectfully to Fifer and left.

'UP THERE? Where Raffaello Riviera banished people to the Winter Storm and created the Firebrand?'

Aldemus looked at Fifer uncertainly, 'are you sure?'

They stood at the bottom of the staircase to the East Tower.

'Well, I have danced in the room where he shot his mother. I would like to see the rest.'

'It's cold up there.'

He took off his jacket and gave it to her, then led the way. She followed, putting it on and shivering slightly. She took in the detail of every floor that they passed with wide eyes. They came out at the top and walked arm in arm around the battlement walkway, taking in the view of the sea and forest, returning to the East Tower, to the highest point where it was possible to stand and look out to sea. She stood as close to the edge as she could. Gulls flew, shots of white against a pale sky with gunmetal clouds. The wind was ice cold and quiet. She stood engulfed in his jacket, her hands hardly visible in the length of the sleeves, refugee like, looking smaller still than her petite frame under its weight.

'Here he created the storm,' she said.

'Yes. Then he fell. He created the Firebrand here too.'

She turned to face him. She hopped from one foot lightly to the other and smiled as if to dance. He was looking for sadness. He thought he saw a glimmer. He could not be sure.

THE NEXT MORNING Louisa sat with Annie in the breakfast room. Annie was segmenting a grapefruit slowly and distractedly, half composing something in her mind, while Louisa methodically updated her red leather book of magicians' abilities. Aldemus entered the room. Louisa looked up and immediately put her pen down. He saw her eyes sparkling in eager anticipation; she had been waiting for him. He looked a little sheepish; he knew what this was about.

'Annie, we had a guest here yesterday,' said Louisa, 'Fifer Savine, a very talented, first order, magician. Our dear brother showed her around. It only took him five hours,' she said with a sardonic smile.

'Five hours!' exclaimed Annie.

Aldemus grinned.

'This castle is steeped in history and beauty. She was fascinated. I felt no need to rush.'

Louisa laughed. Aldemus stretched, moving his arms wide, opening his chest, then he flopped happily into a chair.

'Aldemus! Tell me more. Is she one of your students from the front row?' asked Annie.

'Well...she doesn't really need training,' he replied, and then scowled at Louisa. Louisa laughed. Annie looked at her curiously and Louisa whispered,

'Alligator girl.'

'No!' Annie gasped.

Louisa nodded, 'Oh yes. But she is a Savine, she is his equal, she was playing games to entice him.'

'Equal? My goodness that is the most generous compliment you have ever given me in my entire life. Equal at least. And I am truly enchanted by her,' he said and broke into a wide grin. 'Annie would you please play some music. My heart would like to revel in something beautiful, while I dream in this chair and watch the afternoon float by.' Louisa shook her head. Annie ran to get her guitar.

NATHAN'S LETTER

'*D*id you want me to read through your history of the castle?' asked Esther, walking into Annie's room. Annie was looking out of the window, listening to the music of Lucet Sophia rising up from the courtyard and not her mother. 'Annie, are you still writing the history of the castle? Do you want me to take a look?'

'Uh. Yes! I've not worked on it for ages. There are the letters and notes over there,' she said gesturing to the desk in the corner of her room. Esther walked to the paper-strewn desk and began to gather up the pages. Lucet's violin filled the room and Annie swayed smiling. Esther stood perfectly still, with her back to her daughter. She recognised the hand-writing of Nathan Glass. The ink burned against the page and for a moment she forgot to breathe. She leant against the desk, pulled the letter from Annie's notes and read. Annie hummed to the music. Esther heard Nathan's voice as she read his words; the lines 'I am in your room. I had come to kill you,' circled round and round in her head. Slowly she gathered the papers, gripping them tightly.

'Darling, who have you had letters from so far?'

'Um. Fred, dad, Violet and that's it.'

'When did you last look at these papers?'

'I was working on it until I became more interested in Fred's fish experiments. Then I decided to learn the harpsichord. Then Louisa needed me to count fake magicians. Then I baked some madeleines.'

'When did you last look at these papers?'

Annie looked up, counted on her fingers and then looked perplexed.

'A month ago or maybe two months? I got distracted.'

Esther smiled.

'I'm looking forward to reading this,' she said, walking over to kiss Annie on the forehead, then calmly walking out.

THE MAGIC FOUR sat in the blue velvet chairs in the West Tower. The courtyard had been cleared of all guests. The three Drake children had been sent to Escaville with their good friend Herbert Cavanagan, Violet and Frederick's son. Salem was nervously sweeping the corridors that were too quiet and echoed his every sound.

Horatio read Nathan's letter aloud.

'He wrote this,' said Esther. 'He's alive. He wants us dead.'

'This is a stupid joke. Some idiot trying to create a drama,' said Fred.

'No. It's his handwriting,' said Esther.

'And it sounds like him. Those words. I could hear his voice,' said Violet.

'But it can't be. He's dead! You two told us!' said Fred, his voice raised, as he stared at Esther and Horatio.

'We were wrong,' said Esther.

'So his preparations will be underway. That is what we must assume,' said Horatio.

'Then let's get to work. Find out all we can,' said Violet.

THE HOSING GAMET

*G*eorge, the owner of the Hosing Gamet, was as broad as a bison, with dark eyebrows, that were thick and arched. Warmth could dance and sparkle out of that face like sunlight: eyes full of merriment and a smile as welcoming as open arms. Oh, but be careful, there was always a job to be done, business to be attended to and thirst to be quenched.

The weather in George's face could change in an instant, heralded by a tinkle of broken glass or the slam of a fist into bone. The sunlight would vanish from that face faster than a jaw can bite. The eyebrows would draw together and press down, the left one leading, right one behind, to frame the dark eyes, fierce as hot coals.

Because of George, out of respect for George, the pub with the worst reputation was not a place for too much trouble. Bursts of aggression punctuated the air like laughter, but were fast burning and short lived. A brown wave-like line on the stone arch of the entrance ran over onto the yellow wall with a flash of crimson, a battle scar from an ugly brawl. The mark remained, deliberately, for it served as a warning and reminded George of the sea. Looking at it made her feel calm.

George was not perturbed by the occasional bouts of violence. Angry people did not scare her, she saw their pain, they were as predictable as picnic wasps and with the appropriate distractions, or failing that a good wallop with a shovel, she helped direct them to more restful activity.

It was the quiet ones that scared her, like the young woman with the fingerless gloves who sat comfortably alone. She had a look that George first labelled as 'an air of authority', as she had observed her, each night, for the past few weeks, but dissatisfied with that description, she amended it to 'a look of utter certainty', and a chill ran through her. The young woman regularly met with the twisted looking man in the battered military hat, whom most people avoided. Since her arrival, each time George opened up The Hosing Gamet, she felt a sense of trepidation shrouding her that she could never quite shake off.

The rabble of punters, drawn to and intrigued by the young woman, became different. They talked their tall tales and benign banter and she mostly listened, seldom spoke, but through that quiet confidence she was somehow changing things, creating order and regularity and a greater number of people were seeking her out.

Evening after evening different people would sit with her and talk. New faces appeared every day. She spoke softly, almost in a whisper. George was never quite able to hear what she was saying, only the voices of those around her. The same faces would stand around her, men and women of disrepute, who seemed somehow tamed. Sometimes jewellery was presented to her, beautiful antique pieces. George usually enjoyed people-watching, in the quieter moments, but it now made her feel nervous. Takings were up; the Hosing Gamet had never been so busy. The numbers increased alongside the ringing of the till. The noise rang, like an insistent alarm, in George's ears and increased her fear, which lay blanketed by the business of serving and the absence of watching closely. George was used to keeping an eye on one or two dangerous characters each evening, but the worst ones were returning. An older woman, tonight wearing a black velvet pillbox hat with scarlet netting, was back. She had a smile like a snarl and fiercely alert eyes. George felt colder in her presence and did not like to look into those eyes.

'Oh no. She's not a milliner,' said Gunter, one of the bar workers. He gave an uneasy laugh. 'You don't know her? You surprise me George. You think Rumpkin is unhinged. You don't know the lady? The Lady Dukes.'

And immediately, into George's mind dropped all the dark stories of terror she had heard about Lady Dukes and she held her breath. The drink she was pouring overflowed. She did not notice as the cold liquid ran down her hand and the glass, to soak the floor.

'That's her?' George said amazed and exhaled a long anxious sigh.

One Saturday evening, when the bar was crowded and hot, George realised that everyone she could think of dubious character or deviant magic power was somewhere in the room. It was only when Lady Dukes moved away from the bar and removed her hat of garnet coloured peacock feathers, that George's view was no longer obscured. Then she saw them, all together, in one corner; it was as if they had all come home to roost. George looked at the young woman in the middle, her fingerless gloves now replaced by elegant satin ones. Nimbly she meandered in and out of the bois- terous crowd. She worked the room with an elegant agility, like a satisfied cat purring and rubbing its tail against their legs.

. . .

THE HOSING GAMET had a strong smell, heady and sometimes distinctly unpleasant, but occasionally with a pleasing
familiarity, like peaty woodland on a wet day. Frederick
Cavanagan, who had the nose of a bloodhound, could smell
the Hosing Gamet drifting from the coats and hair of the
patrons walking past him, long before the building came into
sight. It stood before him, indented gold letters against glossy
black, grey stone and arched windows.

Inside was busy. Fred caught sight of his appearance in
the mirror behind the bar and smiled. He liked the fedora. It
made him feel exotic. He never wore hats. He looked around
and realised he was going to fit in easily. Violet was good at
these things. He was glad he had left his disguise up to her.

Tonight he was Jackavoli. Jackavoli, he was delighted to
discover, was good looking. The real Jackavoli was dead. He
had a bad experience with too much absinthe and a rocky
cliff face. He had been a solitary magician, known for practising dramatic magic on cliff edges, late at night, in states of
wild frenzy, rocking-out to his own internal rhythms. He
had been a familiar coastal sight in some parts of the island,
his magic filling the sky with beautiful auroras. Most people,
having observed his dance movements in such chillingly
precarious places, thought it was only a matter of time. His
body was never found. After he vanished, people wondered if
his magic could have been better than his balance. He was
assumed dead, but not confirmed so and the mystery was
well remembered.

In preparation for his disguise, to get into character, Fred
had found a craggy promontory, danced and completely let
go, thrown out the odd laser of colour and thoroughly
enjoyed himself.

The only witness to Jackavoli's demise was a friend of

Violet's, a pirate, who saw him fall, recognised him, tried to revive him, then disposed of him appropriately at sea. A send off where the ocean became momentarily lit with bioluminescence, like a mirror to the night sky filled with stars. The pirate respectfully said a few words and sang him a sea shanty. Jackavoli had no close contacts, but had been regarded as an intelligent, if somewhat unrestrained, magician. Louisa Drake had categorised him as unequivocally 'first order' in her red leather book.

At the bar, a large man with a letterbox smile and three teeth, none of which he minded losing should the situation call for it, slapped Fred on the back and greeted him. Fred recognised him as a notorious card shark and judging by his delight to see Jackavoli, guessed that Jackavoli's last game was not a game that he had won. Fred couldn't decide if this was just a bull of a man or if he was descended from ogres, somewhere along his family tree and mused on this point as he stood talking to him.

Fred looked around and noticed Nicholas Rumpkin in the corner of the room, surrounded by people. He saw the young woman sitting next to him and his faced clouded with concern. He watched her closely as she wrote notes in a small pad. Fred's heart sank. The man with three teeth took a drink over to her. She smiled appreciatively and he began a raucous tale, moving his large frame and blocking her from Fred's view. He sensed the large man to be nervous. When the young woman replied to him, Fred observed him blush like a schoolboy, all the way down his thick neck, but Fred could not hear what she had said.

'Next!' George shouted in his direction and he ordered a drink. 'Not seen you in here for a long time. You here to play cards?' she said, smiling.

'I lost that badly did I?' asked Fred, curiously.

'Yes.'

'Then I am definitely not here to play!' he said and gave a wry smile.

'And you're intrigued too,' she said and looked from him to the corner of the room that he had been observing.

'Everyone comes to meet the General. Good for business.' Then she lowered her voice, 'But bad news. Seems to be organising, planning and recruiting for something, hence the name. Magicians from all over keep appearing. A troop now, and we're not talking acrobats.'

George shrugged, then looked at him uncertainly, changed the subject and spoke at her usual volume.

'You're magic, right? Must be with a hat like that.'

Fred smiled and doffed his fedora.

'Totally. Minor magic. Card tricks. Never has an opponent lost.'

She smiled at his joke.

'So what's it all about with the General?' he asked.

Again, she looked at him uncertainly, before fixing him with a firm stare and speaking.

'The General is selling a ghost.'

Fred looked puzzled as she continued, 'It's either a very good con or Nathan Glass isn't dead.'

Fred wrinkled his face in disbelief.

'Plenty of people are convinced,' she said.

'Worse than I thought,' said Fred.

He looked over at the young woman. His senses must be dulling; she had always seemed genuine, he had not seen this coming. He felt sick. The satin hands that rested on the shoulders of others reached out as the battered military hat was passed to her. She took it gracefully and placed it on her head, perfectly, like a crown.

'Those eyes should be blue fire,' said George, as Fifer's warm brown eyes lit up in the dark corner of the room. 'Her Savine ancestors were all taken into the Winter Storm, marked by their ice-blue eyes and prevented from returning by Raffaello's Firebrand. Which no one has seen since she and her dark-eyed mother arrived. Perhaps they slew the dragon? If they did, if they can destroy the Scion's greatest magic…no wonder that lot are seeking her out.'

Fred finished his drink in one and made his way over to her.

'I'm JACKAVOLI,' said Fred to Fifer as he sat down opposite her and removed his hat.

'He's dead,' she said.

'They say that about all the best magicians,' he replied.

Fifer smiled and then eyed him suspiciously.

'What do you mean?'

'Nathan Glass,' he replied.

'He burned out,' she said.

'He created the darkness and lived on. That shouldn't be possible, but it is. He's the Scion.'

'Pah, conspiracy theory,' she replied. He now had her complete attention. Fred shook his head,

'No.'

Nicholas Rumpkin sidled over to them and prodded him on the shoulder.

'Jackavoli, you must be a friend of the Drakes, I bet you hang out in the castle courtyard making magic, because no one has seen you in here for a very long time,' he said. Fred ignored him and continued to look at Fifer.

'You're an interesting choice for his henchman,' he observed, tilting his head and looking at her inquisitively. 'Sure, I go to the castle. Friend is a stronger word than I would use; but I am interested in magic and in power. How is Aldemus Drake…General?'

Her eyes widened in surprise, amazed that he could have

observed her and Aldemus at the castle, without her ever noticing him. She sat perfectly still, staring at him intently. Fred felt a dismay descending, that he was careful not to show. He wondered if he had gone too far, pushed her to doubt him. As he looked unflinchingly into her eyes, he realised how much he had underestimated her. She clasped her hands together and broke into a wide smile.

'Coming along nicely. You've got to be careful who you can trust,' she said.

Fifer was impressed by Jackavoli and had decided that he could be useful to her. Fred smiled back.

'Indeed. I'd like to keep on the right side of the Scion. Nathan has my allegiance, should he require it.'

'Allegiance to what?'

'That's what I want you to tell me.'

IN THE DARKNESS

*N*athan had once felt compassion deeply in his heart. So it was with ease, from the moment he first met Fifer in the darkness, after Betty had ticked her name, that he found the words and gestures to make her feel comfortable. She was brave, younger and more accomplished than most of the magicians who dared to enter. Just as he had been, when he first entered the courtyard of Stonerock castle many years before. She drew close over time. In his blackening heart he felt little emotion; other than mild satisfaction that what he needed to achieve was being achieved. He provided friendship; she hoped for more. He knew how to keep the light of love burning brightly, knew that hope was a driving force.

When they danced in the darkness he thought how alike the movements on the dance floor were to the game he was playing, to the things he was setting in motion. To the figments it looked natural, effortless. It flowed in unexpected ways, with twists and turns and an ending that was always coming.

A few weeks after they had first met, Fifer and Nathan sat in the darkness with their backs to the flame room door. He held her, stroked her hair and felt her soften in his arms. He listened to the story of her history; she opened up to him like a water lily in the sun. Her tears wet his shirt as she talked about her family, life in the Winter Storm, injustices they had suffered and the terrible deaths met by those who had tried to return to the island. A soft rhythmic sound, only just discernible in the background, helped her breathing deepen and allowed her to relax. It was the sound of huge lungs expanding, filling with air and then slowly exhaling. The Firebrand asleep behind the door at which they sat, gently warming their backs.

NATHAN LEFT THE DARKNESS TWICE, once on the night of the winter ball and once before for a single evening, alone. The first time he left he felt emboldened by Fifer's fearlessness, as determined as the look in her eyes, with the unwavering belief that she could escape her past. Time with Fifer, feeling her admiration and energy boosted him. A spark of courage ascended within him, tiny and glistening. Encouragement, such a meek word for the lion it enables to roar.

One evening, under the cover of nightfall, he returned to the castle and stood in the courtyard, in the exact place where his heart had once broken, to lay the past to rest. But rising up from his heart was the murderous desire to destroy everything around him. He observed it, held it back. He wanted to walk away from the feeling. Instead he walked through the wall and sought to find the room where he used to create dreams with Esther and Violet. A place of happier times, when he was different, when life was different. He found it, but it was no longer the same. It was Annie's bedroom now. He saw his favourite chair by her writing desk. He saw Annie asleep and the paintings on the wall. He stared at the paintings, expected his anger to ignite, but he just felt floored by the certainty of Horatio's deception. He sat down in the chair and wrote Annie the letter.

THE GENERAL

*V*iolet, Esther and Horatio were sitting in the blue velvet chairs around the table. Fred came into the room at uncharacteristic speed, with a look of consternation that immediately made the other three stop talking and give him their full attention. He was too agitated to sit down.

'Fifer Savine is the General. Nathan's general. He will exact his revenge here, at the winter ball in front of everyone. He wants an audience. And in that audience will be many of his supporters. Some of whom will come as a surprise to us, no doubt. It is difficult to know who to trust,' said Fred.

'Revenge for what?' said Violet and Esther at the same time.

Fred shrugged.

'It's unclear. She said, 'The castle belongs to the Scion. His power must be seen. The magic four destroyed. He will take his rightful place.'

'Rightful place? That's the motivation of a banished child of the Winter Storm. Not Nathan,' said Esther.

'He was never interested in the castle, in status. That's you Horatio, that's what you want,' said Violet.

'Fifer?' said Horatio in disbelief.

'Don't underestimate her,' said Fred.

'This makes no sense. We were friends with Nathan! We were all friends!' said Violet rising to walk around the room.

'He is not of sound mind. He chose to leave. We couldn't entice him back,' said Horatio.

'He cannot be reasoned with. Something has happened to him. His heart has gone the way of the many hearts we observed together. There is always a trigger. In fish it is an attack. It cannot be reversed, once the first drop enters the blood. He will have felt it and known what it meant. Maybe that is why he left, when he felt his heart going black. We watched it, simulated it, now he is living it.'

'Cannot be reversed? You're certain?' asked Esther.

'In fish and mere mortals yes, but not in magic fish or magic mortals; it's very unlikely,' Fred replied.

'What happens then? He will become like the Bad-Freddie fish?' asked Esther.

'Or like Raffaello. The Winter Storm, the Firebrand, destruction,' said Violet.

'Gradually, like the Bad-Freddie fish, yes. His power will turn against him or against others, the drive to destroy will begin to dominate him.'

'But there is always the white speck,' said Esther.

'Yes,' Fred replied.

'Good or bad?' asked Violet.

'Of that I cannot be certain,' replied Fred.

Horatio stood and walked around the room and said,

'In the darkness he meets a young woman with a purpose, who like him, knows isolation. She wants the magic of her family, held back for generations, to be finally recognised, displayed even. She saves him from himself. She helps him to take aim, to try and prove himself as the Scion. It's her history leading them to this.'

'Or maybe it is driven by him, not her,' said Fred. He looked around the room at the others, observing them closely. 'If he is coming for revenge, then he feels harmed, betrayed.'

'Poor Aldemus. He's besotted,' said Esther, putting her hands to her face, 'What is the petite evil going to do to him? To my beautiful boy,' she asked fluctuating between despair and vexation.

'I think she's done with him. She needed a way into the castle, insight into us. She'll only come back when it's time,' said Violet.

'Three weeks,' said Horatio.

'Do we cancel it? Close down the castle?' asked Frederick.

'No,' said the others, at the same time.

'We let him come,' said Horatio.

'Was she suspicious of you Fred?' asked Violet.

'No. I did Jackavoli proud. On the contrary, she recruited me. I'll be in charge of the traitors that will cover the West Wing. To hunt us down.'

They all stared in horror at Fred.

'Who are they?' asked Horatio.

'There is Rumpkin, Lady Dukes, some minor magic nuisances. The rest will be revealed on the night; Fifer is not taking any chances.'

SECRETS, be they ugly and choking or pretty and small, are not happily bottled up. They like to be looked at and people like to parade them, to at least one other person. A person who can completely contain the jerking ogre of a secret is a rare and true friend, but what else may lie in the vault of that mind? How worried should you be?

The magic four knew Nathan was coming. They had a plan. A secret. They could talk to each other and did so every day, perched in the cobalt velvet chairs of the North Tower. They went over and over the details. Their strategy swivelled like a lasso with four magic intellects cavorting, in perfect time. They made sure the rhythm was right to synchronise all the movements and magic they needed to save themselves, their families and the castle.

Then they were all so fed up of discussing it that they could no longer bear the sight of each other. Esther went to do some gardening and took a large pick axe. Frederick Cavanagan headed to the bakers' giving himself permission to eat anything he desired. Horatio went for a swim in the lake and Violet walked the entire coastline that fringed the southern forest.

Horatio did not tell anyone beyond the magic four, as he did not think for one moment that the plan could be improved or that anyone beyond them could be trusted. He considered the plan to be flawless. Violet did not believe flawless existed, not even in magic. It was Horatio's certainty that made Violet want to seek a confidante outside of the circle, but she resisted, until the night of the winter ball.

Esther had moments when she was tempted to tell Louisa, but she could never tell Aldemus and he would never forgive her for telling Louisa, so she remained quiet. Even in the moments when she feared that they would need all the magic help that they could get, even that of their own children, she resisted the temptation to enlist their help. Her love for them was as great as the terror that now swam amongst her thoughts. Thoughts that wearied her and strengthened her resolve to destroy Nathan.

Salem had to know parts of the plan, he had his instructions and they relied on him to follow them. He got glimpses of it, could probably deduce more, but even he sensed that knowing would not benefit anyone.

Frederick's closest friend beyond the magic four was Periwinkle Penhaligon the logician and mathematician. Peri made his living through his skill in these areas. Magic for Peri was all about numbers and their patterns, which fell elegantly into his mind and gave him answers. He created mind-blowing calculations that allowed him to predict the outcomes of events with incredible accuracy, so it was not long before others sought his help and were willing to pay for it. He was delighted when Violet created the Waiting Room and had twice cleaned out the bookmakers at the Grand National during his summer holidays. After bothering him weekly with random and irrelevant questions, for which Peri did the appropriate maths, Frederick came in to his shop and just sat down.

'Not you again,' said Peri smiling. Peri had an infectious smile, was beautifully freckled, with orange hair as vibrant as a tropical flower, always a picture of cheerfulness. Frederick rested his elbow on his knee and leant forward to place his forehead in the palm of his hand. 'Oh dear, Frederick. What's Violet done now?'

Frederick shook his head, then looked up.

'It's not Violet. Do you have any appointments soon?'

'No. Just browsers, who might come in.'

Fred lowered his head, shifted from side to side then looked up again.

'How many magicians are needed to take down Nathan Glass?'

'Isn't he dead?' asked Peri, mystified. 'And isn't Horatio Drake the greatest magician of his generation?' he added with a smile. Frederick did not smile back and Peri's own smile quickly vanished. 'You mean can it be done if he's alive and he's the Scion? Can the four of you do it?' Frederick went white. 'You don't have to answer that Fred. If you really need the answer to that question, then I want to know as little as possible.' Peri began searching in a tall mahogany cabinet, through small, brass labelled drawers. 'I have worked it out before…' He found what he was looking for and flicked through it.

'Well?'

'All four of you, I believe it is possible, but there is no room for error. Three of you, very difficult, it may be the last thing you ever do. Two of you, no.'

'Right.'

'Give him as little time as possible. The quicker you act, the better your chances.'

The bell tinkled as the door to the shop opened and a woman in a large hat adorned with the carcass of a small, silver-plated, crab appeared. Fred thanked Peri and held the door for Lady Dukes as he was leaving. Her appearance was not good news. Trouble seemed to be crawling out of the woodwork and infesting everywhere. Fred had always seen the good in people. He could count on one hand the people he had experienced in his entire life whom he believed were truly terrible. Seeing most of them reappear over the last three weeks made his heart sink and his skin tingle with cold anxiety.

BEFORE THE WINTER BALL

Painted green with flourishes of red and gold around the windows, the wooden building stood cheerfully amidst the drizzle that had turned the forest grey. Above the scarlet door in swirling lettering was written Cavanagans. The Drake children stood sullen in the rain, having been firmly swept out of the castle on their parents' orders. When Violet opened the door only a damp Annie managed a weak half smile. They traipsed inside. Louisa and Aldemus slumped into chairs next to Herbert Cavanagan, who looked similarly despondent.

'There will be other parties,' said Violet.

'You look nice,' said Annie admiring Violet's full-length emerald green evening gown.

'Yes, enjoy yourself in our home dear Violet,' said Aldemus sarcastically. He softened slightly as Herbert passed him a drink.

'Your parents would not do this without good reason,' said Violet.

'But that is what they and you have neglected to tell us, the reason,' said Herbert.

'They know how much we were looking forward to it,' said Annie.

'It's getting late. Let's talk about this tomorrow. For now you have Cavanagans entirely at your disposal, to have as much fun as you like, with no adults in the way,' said Violet.

'We thought you'd be pleased!' said Fred entering the room. His jovial demeanour was greeted with silence. He helped Violet into her coat.

'Aldemus, it is your birthday soon. Then you shall have an amazing party that will surpass this. Your father is already making plans,' said Fred.

'You think we can't be trusted with something,' said Herbert, looking at his father.

'That's not true Herb,' said Fred, opening the door.

'Enough,' said Violet, 'we must go. Have a nice evening.'

When the door had closed Louisa said,

'It's your fault Aldemus. They want to keep you away from Fifer. Mother referred to her as the petite evil when talking to Salem this morning about table plans. We all have to suffer as a result of your poor choice in women.'

Aldemus glared at her.

'That's not true! It's not that. Only you think that. Fifer isn't even going. I asked her to be my guest and she said no,' he replied.

'If it's not that, then something is wrong. Something is up,' said Louisa.

Aldemus, Herbert and Annie began a game of cards.

'I'm so upset. I spent weeks on the music, none of which I'll hear. I was going to perform and they've given my slot to Lucet! Chosen him over their own daughter!'

Aldemus and Herb shook their heads in disbelief as they looked at their cards. Louisa stood looking out of the window and watched Frederick and Violet walk into the forest. Just before they were out of sight, Violet turned, looked back and opened and closed her left hand twice.

Louisa's jaw dropped, she stared at the others, then looked back through the window and said with incredulity,

'I know what she has done!' The others looked up in alarm. 'Violet has just thrown down a force field. They've locked us in!' she said.

'No way!' said Herbert, jumping up.

'To what range?' said Aldemus joining him.

'Can't tell. To the edge of the forest? She's circled the building.'

They all raced outside. Aldemus and Herbert ran forward a few paces, only to smash into an invisible wall, and then step back in pain, nursing body parts that had made contact with the force field. Interested, Louisa placed her hands gently against it, climbing them up like a mine artist. It felt cool and smooth, detectable only through touch, yet the rain passed through it, wetting her hands.

'Perhaps it is a test?' said Aldemus, rubbing his wrist, 'maybe they want us to prove our magic and break it, then they'll let us go to the ball!'

'Oh yes! That makes sense! It must be a challenge, a game!' said Annie.

'I doubt it. They've lost all playfulness recently. Their grave faces, always so preoccupied,' said Louisa.

'Yes.' said Herbert, Louisa's description resonating with him. 'I'm certain that they genuinely do not want us to go. It's not a test.' He sighed. Then, as if to cheer himself, he added, 'but it might be fun to have a go at breaking it!' A mischievous expression lit his face. Aldemus grinned. Annie clapped her hands in excitement.

As soon as Violet was inside the castle, she felt the need to be outside. To rid herself of the feeling of claustrophobia before the evening unfolded. The beauty and opulent decoration was lost on her. She wanted to feel the elements. So she left unnoticed and darted down towards the rocky shore. Once out of sight, she lingered in the night air, running through the plan in her mind as she listened to the rushing of the waves. Her breath came out in elongated sighs as she walked towards the rocks and looked out to sea, letting the breeze blow her hair from her face. She drew her coat around her emerald gown and clutched her evening bag with icy fingers.

She did not see him. He sat quietly on the limestone rock, his dark curls and tuxedo a twilight camouflage. Marley Jaker was examining various watches of intricate design, attached to wrap of fabric. He turned on hearing her approach and she jumped backwards in surprise.

'Sorry, didn't mean to frighten you,' he said.

'Marley Jaker! '

'Violet!'

'I never knew that pirates could look so distinguished!'

He smiled in delight and dusted imaginary specks from his shoulders.

Violet laughed, 'I am a little edgy tonight. What have you got there?'

Marley's eyes sparkled.

'A sea witch gave them to me.'

Violet raised an eyebrow.

'Hmm…'

'You think I stole them.'

'I didn't think there were such things as sea witches. I thought they were an excuse for bad weather.'

'That doesn't surprise me. How often have you been to sea?'

'…Does canoeing count?'

Marley pretended to look aghast.

'Sea witches are not witches you see, except in bad weather. Most of the time they float on the ocean, a languid, translucent turquoise. Where the sea is blue there are none, but the sea is rarely true blue; there's usually a tinge of green somewhere. They are peaceful mostly and only rise with the storms.'

'Really?'

'Aye. I get on well with sea witches. They know I'm a honourable captain, not a common pirate.'

He grinned again. She looked at his face more closely.

'Yes, Marley. I know all about you.'

'I'm an uncommon pirate. I'm like you Violet and I know all about you too.'

She smiled again.

'How are you like me?'

The zip on the clutch bag she held, opened slowly and three small, exotic coloured birds flew out. They landed on the rocks, sang out at her, then disappeared in silent fireworks, shimmering against the dark. She gave him a warm smile and sat down next to him.

'I'm surprised that Horatio invited you, my friend, even if you are real magic.'

'I'm Esther's guest. '

'Ah.'

She shivered, picked up a handful of rough stones and began to throw them one by one out towards the water. Then thought, with a colder shiver, of something that the magic four had overlooked.

'Jackavoli,' she said quite suddenly, turning to look again at Marley.

'God rest his soul,' said Marley, waiting for her to continue.

'Who knows he's dead?' she said with a sense of urgency.

'You, me and whoever you've told? You said there was no family.'

'There isn't. And no one else knows?'

'No. A few fish maybe. What's going on?'

'Jackavoli… will be at the ball tonight,' she said matter of factly.

Marley raised an eyebrow.

'At the ball…'

'Except, it will actually be Fred,' said Violet pulling a pained expression.

'Your Fred?'

'Yes. Well at times he will be Fred and at times Jackavoli.'

'Ok,' said Marley, awaiting further explanation that did not come. Aware of Violet's discomfort, he smiled and said, 'I'm sure he will looking dashing in the Fedora.' Looking anguished Violet began,

'I need you…'

'To keep your secrets?'

'Yes.'

'Not a problem.'

She exhaled in relief and relaxed.

'You can talk to me if you like.'

'What?'

'About what's troubling you.'

INSIDE THE DARKNESS, the area where Betty sat was cosy and welcoming, bathed in warm light from the brass desk lamp, the porcelain lamps on the armoire behind her and the large candles in gilded sconces either side of the contemplation room door. She watched as Nathan waited for Fifer, slightly nervous as he checked his watch. Betty smiled to herself, knowing that Fifer was never late. Then they both heard Fifer's fast and light footsteps coming down the dark corridor. She emerged from the black hallway in vivid colour, a burst of bougainvillea-bloom despite the darkness. Betty gasped and clasped her hands together in excitement.

'Gorgeous!' she said, unable to contain herself.

Nathan greeted Fifer and stood before her in his tuxedo. His brown hair had flecks of grey. She looked youthful, beautiful and radiant. He felt the years between them. He looked at her, acutely aware that he was older, tainted, grizzled, battered by life and preserved by darker forces. Her heart open and overflowing, his heart contaminated, held in aspic. He remembered when he was once like her, recalling this without emotion, but with great clarity. For a moment he pictured the tiny white light within his heart. Untainted or orchestrating it all? He cared not which anymore. The image faded quickly. Tonight his magic would roar.

'I think he scrubs up quite nicely too,' Betty said proudly.

Fifer moved to sit on her desk and they were both looking at him smiling. He smiled back uncomfortably, almost bashful.

'So beautiful. Dazzling in your beauty Fifer. Vibrant, youthful, perfect,' he said. She revelled in the compliments. Nathan did not fear Fifer's rejection. He recognised the look in her eyes and knew how malleable she was. She took his arm, captivated by his amber eyes that looked more focused tonight than she had ever seen.

'Yes, but not so young,' she replied, 'and all beauty fades,' she added softly, smiled and for a split second became a shrunken, withered old crone, in a worn out gown, beaming toothless at him, before returning to her immaculate evening attire, feline eyes sparkling. He laughed and she laughed too. A welcome respite from the precision perfect planning that circulated in her mind for constant inspection.

'You are delightful,' he said.

'Tonight you will show them. I believe in you, Nathan Glass.'

He took her hand. Betty smiled in contentment at the happy moment. Fifer had really seemed to come alive, she thought and Nathan, although she did not want to get her hopes up, seemed to be moving towards happiness or at least some level of satisfaction. Nathan and Fifer said goodbye and walked away down the dark corridor, the vivid colour of Fifer's cerise dress vanishing into black.

MILLICENT WAS in the blacksmith's shop messing around with a broomstick, amusing herself by making it fly, imagining the embarrassment on Fifer's face if she were to fly past her on it. She laughed aloud and it sounded a bit like a cackle, which made her laugh all the more. She was experimenting to make it more comfortable to ride on, trying various objects as seats: an atlas with an oven glove, a bag of soil wrapped in a leather apron, a folded piece of old carpet.

The town was quiet and when she stopped to think about it, she realised it must be the evening of the winter ball. Her invitation stood on the mantelpiece. She had wondered if she should go, but Fifer told her there would be ice caves, that it would be extremely cold and Horatio Drake would be sitting in a throne like chair and suddenly her own company had seemed much more appealing. She was going to go for a night walk, which she regularly did, when the idea of making the broomstick fly became irresistible. And so it was that she found herself flying witch-like around the almost empty town of Escaville, on a seat fashioned from an iron trivet in a tea cosy stuffed with rag. Yes, she could have magicked something better, but it was fun to build it with her hands.

'Wheeee!' She went up and down, up and down, twanging a few street lamps as she went, until she could maintain steady flight. She shot around town, window level at first, having a good look inside the empty houses, and then on a whim started righting the odd slipped roof tile if she spotted one and if she liked the inhabitants. She got a bit carried away fixing the baker's guttering until the trivet-tea-cosy seat thoroughly numbed her bony backside. Then out of necessity and for her own amusement she used magic to create a firm cushion in a tangerine tiger print with a beaded tassel trim.

She flew over the southern forest, with its treetops gently rising and falling like a black ocean, and decided that even she did not fancy venturing in there tonight, in the dark. She headed for the coast to test out her flying ability, skimming as close to the water as she could, not intending to get her feet wet and realising she was not as accomplished as she had hoped. Slightly wet-socked and disappointed she flew up high at breakneck speed and took in the view of the whole island. The cold wind shot through her wet toes like lightning. She saw to her surprise a warm light glowing in the northern forest, on the other side of Escaville, a beacon against the dark night. It must be Cavanagans, she thought. She had assumed Frederick, Violet and Herbert would be at the castle, that no one would be there. The thought of a roaring fire and piano music made her dive the broomstick down to see if anyone was.

As she got closer she could see that most of the lights were on and figures were moving about outside. She sped up. She could not see the force field as she flew towards it and smashed into it. Then she lay unconscious on the ground, her eyes closed.

'Whoa! She could be really hurt,' said Louisa.

'So painful! And she looked so happy too,' said Annie.

Herbert Cavanagan and the Drakes were banging on the

force field and jumping around, trying to get Millicent's attention.

'Wake up! Wake up!' Aldemus bellowed.

'She's out cold,' said Herbert.

'She's our way out,' said Aldemus.

Millicent's eyes opened briefly. Her mouth and fingers moved as she uttered hardly decipherable complaining sounds. 'What do we tell her? I'm not sure she likes our family,' Aldemus added.

'A Cavanagan, that's what you need,' said Herbert, in his rich, resonant voice.

Millicent's eyes opened again and they all shouted and jumped frantically. She reached out a sinewy arm to drag the tiger cushion and put it under her head, then closed her eyes again. Annie went into Cavanagans and came out with a guitar. She began to play and sing, standing as close to Millicent as she could. Millicent's body softened into the ground and the corners of her mouth turned up, her right foot began to move in time to the beat.

'Louder!' cried Aldemus and by the next chord he had turned the guitar into an electric one so the sound could blast out. Still the foot tapped and the smile rose, but the eyes stayed closed. Half way through the second song, with Millicent's eyes firmly shut, Louisa clicked her fingers and the cushion became a speaker. Quickly a startled Millicent sat bolt upright, looking into the smiling eyes of Herbert Cavanagan.

'Millicent, it's ok; we'll look after you. You flew into a force field. Come in, sit down, rest a while here. Oh, wait, there's a force field. Could you help us with that?'

Millicent rubbed her head and looked at him curiously.

'Why is there one? Who put it there?'

'My mother.'

'Ah, I see,' she replied and eyed him suspiciously, until her eyes came to rest on the view through the open door of Cavanagans, where she saw a comfortable chair and the warm flickering light from the fire.

'She's testing us, seeing how good we are, we're still learning, but we need to join her at the castle for the ball and we don't want to be late,' said Herbert.

'Ah yes, the ball,' she replied, hardly listening, as she realised she could not feel her toes, just pain that fitted with the memory of where they once were. She was cold, colder than she had been for a long time. I want to be by that fire, she thought and that thought kept repeating loudly and impatiently. Any concern about why Violet might be locking them in began to diminish.

'We are so close, but we can't break through, could you help us?' asked Annie, crossing her fingers tightly behind her back and holding her breath. Aldemus bit his lip. They all looked at Millicent eagerly, waiting motionless, held in suspense.

'What force field?' said Millicent, who stood up and walked straight to the front door. They gasped, cried out in excitement, jumped and whooped.

'Thank you! Make yourself at home!' shouted Herbert as he and the others charged out in the direction of the castle.

IN THE DARKNESS, the artist spilled a third pot of red paint and cursed. Betty had left her glasses in an odd place and forgotten where exactly that was. She put four sugars into the artist's black coffee, which would usually make him volcanic, but he did not notice. Other figments who usually glided were stumbling; their sounds were discordant and alarming. The Firebrand's tail beat against the flame room walls.

Nathan and Fifer had left for the ball; they had been gone

some time. The Firebrand was hyper-alert when Nathan left the darkness and only relaxed on his return. Tonight it had seen Fifer. It glimpsed her brown eyes and evening dress of pink ruffles, through the closing door. It remembered her. Fifer did not see the dragon. A residue of its lethal former self was ignited. There was an odd sensation in its chest, as if its heart was being scrunched into a tight ball. An echo of the confusion it had felt many years ago when Claudia Savine had held up Millicent, her brown-eyed baby; a replay of the tension it felt when it saw Millicent and Fifer arrive on the island. The dragon scraped its talons against the floor. These were bad feelings, which it knew led to relentless misery. 'Nathan saved me, brought me here,' was all it could think and all it thought, on repeat; sat on its haunches, listening, focused on the one thing that mattered to it most, protecting Nathan.

THE WINTER BALL

*W*hen Fifer and Nathan arrived at the castle they paused in the entrance hall and looked up to the glittering aqua-light of the ice cave above, which seemed to go on into infinity. Quickly, Fifer looked straight ahead again: winter was not a season for sentiment. Nathan continued looking upward and felt the illusion of snow falling on his face, cold but not wet. He smiled as frosted mauve and lemon flowers appeared on the stone walls around him crisp and sharp. He felt the chill and recognised Esther's work as the intricate snowflakes fell, evaporating just before they touched the ground.

Fifer ignored the cashmere stole that appeared in the air before her. A silver grey hat appeared before Nathan, he smiled and reached out for it, soft as angel hair. On his touch it turned into an arctic fox with piercing eyes, it leapt in the air and vanished before it landed. Fifer tugged at his hand and they moved from the aqua light of the ice into the warmth of the castle, its oven breath greeting them with rich smells of rosemary, mandarin and musky vanilla as they walked along. How she loved the warmth, she felt its embrace down the corridors and as they entered the great hall.

Despite herself, Fifer was struck by the beauty of the room, golden ivy, icicle chandeliers glistening and music with a beat as strong as her anxious heart. For a split second she wanted to melt into the room, dance and be with Nathan without an agenda of revenge, without an agenda at all. She put her arm around his waist.

At that moment, the magic four were variously, in deep conversation, listening intently or laughing in good humour. As soon as Nathan stepped foot in the room, they were instantly aware of his presence. It was as if their ears pricked up at exactly the same moment, hyper-alert to the proximity of danger, or prey. They did not break eye contact or break off their sentences. The world kept turning in the same way, but they had all shifted subtly, to be able to see him, the entrance always in their peripheral vision. Esther was the one closest to him.

Fifer's wistful reverie of being with Nathan was soon over. Her wishes evaporated like the snowflakes that never touched the ground as Esther Drake came into sight. It was not because he pulled away from her; it was the way he looked at Esther. Nothing he could say could change that. Fifer had seen it and it could not be unseen. His face became one she did not recognise, softer, yet afraid. She felt him tremble and tried to pull him gently away. He resisted without noticing, without acknowledging, his mind was flying back through the years the old feelings rushing through his whole body. All he wanted, in that moment, was to be with her.

Esther turned, recognised him, smiled and immediately came over. She looked radiant, harmony in motion as she came towards them. Her whole demeanour was genial and welcoming. But it made Fifer feel cold, cold like the old days, as if iced water was trickling through her veins, expanding outwards, sinking her.

Mesmerising eyes, Fifer noticed as she finally raised hers to meet Esther's. They were light, bright and icy, in contrast to everything else about her. Fifer thought this as she looked into them and did not hear what Esther said. In her mind she was pushing her warmth, her words back, back away. It was only when Esther walked away that Fifer realised that it had been a long time since anyone had spoken. Nathan stood watching Esther and the world seemed to slip away, she was not sure if he was slipping from her or if she was slipping from everything. The room seemed to spin, although neither she nor Nathan had moved and he was standing close.

Nathan looked around the full span of the room, taking in all the guests, many of whom were listed in his mind, many of whom nodded discreetly in his direction. He snapped back into the present. He squeezed Fifer's hand.

'What you have done is amazing, thank you,' he said.

'I hope I have proved myself to you. I want you to see what I am capable of and perhaps what we could be capable of…together.'

Her eyes went to the floor and her gaze trailed around her feet. He said nothing, watched her become more uncomfortable as she stood before him. He feigned confusion, but observed her closely intrigued by his results, 'I have surprised you,' she laughed nervously. 'I suppose I should be glad of that. Not many people can, I suppose. I had hope, foolish hope, I thought you might have seen me differently, but it will always be her.'

'You are a child of the Winter Storm. You're different Fifer. I have seen you in action. You're…'

She stood up straighter, her petite stature seeming to tower over him. Her fawn-like eyes wide open as she looked at him questioningly.

'You think I am unable to feel? Incapable of love? Evil?'

'Like me.'

There was hardness in his voice, a searing finality to his tone. Fifer felt suddenly exposed and defenceless. To her alarm and horror tears welled immediately. She fought to hold them back. He looked at her uncomprehendingly. She quickly composed herself, smoothing out all traces of vulnerability.

'Tonight will be everything you hoped. You will show them who you are. She will see you.'

The corners of his mouth turned up and he eyed her with suspicion. Her focus had returned. She looked at him, her expression completely neutral. He placed his arm around her.

'In my heart there is an empty space where she once was. Just empty space. The rest is black.'

Her face had regained the dispassionate authority of the General. Her eyes blazed with unflinching determination. She strode down the corridor throwing out spells and silent orders to the other traitors. As she blinked a single tear, too late to suppress, escaped, travelled across her cheek and ran down the side of her face. The side he could not see as she walked away.

HERBERT CAST an invisibility spell over the four of them as the castle came into sight, lit by flaming torches. They ran to the entrance and discovered the challenge of being coordinated and unheard if guests were close by. Louisa and Aldemus's frustration grew quickly alongside Annie and Herbert's distraction. In the entrance hall Annie wandered off as soon as she heard the music. Herbert was mesmerised by the beauty of the ice carvings and frozen fountains in the courtyard and gazed without listening. Louisa and Aldemus argued in brief bursts of succinct commands, when the moment allowed, or nudged and elbowed each other when guests were passing by.

'Mother created this ice cave, it's so cool!' said Annie, her voice now some distance above them.

'Get back down now!' said Louisa

'Herb where are you?' asked Aldemus.

'Here.'

And before they had travelled the short distance to the great hall gallery, Louisa had taken some decorative golden ivy and tied their wrists together. The golden strands floated in a line of ghostly handcuffs as they moved carefully, past the open doors of the great hall, further along the corridor towards the gallery staircase. The castle teemed with magic effects to delight and mystify the guests at every turn. No one noticed the moving golden foliage that bound the friends together. Three silent snowy owls gliding above them, leaving trails of tiny silver stars provided ample distraction.

The gallery was empty, the dark wood polished to a warm sheen. They climbed to the back row, to seek a high vantage point and to avoid being heard. The ivy fell to the floor as they sat down. They could see the Harleshamp band on stage opposite them and the guests starting to take their seats for dinner.

'There's Fifer,' said Louisa, as Fifer walked happily along arm in arm with Nathan. She voiced what her brother had also seen but was too furious to articulate. Although Aldemus was invisible, they could all picture his darkened features exactly.

'Who is she with? Who is that man?' asked Annie.

'I've never seen him before,' said Louisa.

'Not in Cavanagans either,' added Herbert.

'She's fawning all over him,' said Annie, 'the petite evil. That's what I heard mother call her.'

When the majority of guests were seated Horatio stood up and called the hall to attention. Poems of joy appeared in calligraphic script on the stone walls behind him as he gave a welcome to all,

'And a special mention to an old friend,' Horatio looked to the man that they did not recognise and raised his champagne flute, 'who has returned to the castle after a long time in the wilderness. Ladies and gentleman I would like to propose a toast to Nathan Glass.' Fifer put her arm around Nathan and rubbed his shoulder reassuringly. Nathan gave a modest smile as all drinks were raised and all eyes were on him.

'Almost as old as father,' spat Aldemus.

'Not quite, he's a good five or six years younger I'd say,' said Louisa, then anticipated and dodged an invisible shove from Aldemus, 'He is the magician who created the darkness. He is supposed to be dead,' Louisa whispered.

Horatio sat down. The band began to play. People could not settle to eat. The room was restless. Guests talked too quickly, laughed too eagerly, repeatedly got up and moved. Most plates were untouched. Guests changed seats; swapped back, adjusted ties, smoothed dresses, fidgeted, until eventually everyone was seated. Horatio tucked into his steak with a voracious appetite.

'That man just took a watch!' cried Annie.

'Where?' asked Louisa.

'Nathan?' asked Herbert.

'No! That man, he arrived late, standing up, further along, with dark curly hair. I don't recognise him either,' she replied.

'Marley Jaker. Pirate. Father deplores, Violet adores,' said Louisa.

'Good magician,' said Aldemus.

'He's a thief!' replied Annie, 'See and see again, he took her necklace! We must stop him.'

Annie pointed and as she did so her hand materialised from the invisibility spell. A gesture cast in indignation now translucent and eerily detached. Slowly her wrist and lower arm appeared. She gasped. 'What shall we do?'

'Keep watching him,' said Louisa.

'No! What shall we do about no longer being invisible?'

Annie turned to see Herbert and her siblings materialising before her like apparitions.

'No one is looking up here. I think we'll be fine,' said Louisa calmly.

'We can smile and wave at them. Look he did it again!' said Aldemus.

'Thief!' said Annie scornfully.

Marley almost sat down in empty seat after seat, then stood as if he had made a mistake, smiling, apologising and greeting the guests near him.

'And again! He's taking antique jewellery. Shall we stop him?' said Aldemus.

'No. Let's watch him,' said Louisa.

'He's taking talismans. Jewellery with a magic charge. Look how she misses her necklace now, that look of fright,' said Herbert.

'Yes. Perspiration, paler now,' said Louisa.

'That's more than a lucky charm,' said Aldemus.

'Protection?' asked Herbert.

'Weapon,' said Louisa, 'he's disarming them.'

'That doesn't sound good,' said Annie in alarm.

'He's approaching non-magic or minor magic only. Watch, he won't touch Dukes,' said Aldemus, 'he'll go for the woman with the orange flower next.'

Marley smiled at Lady Dukes and gave a deferential bow,

walked straight past her, past Nathan and Fifer and settled next to a woman wearing a persimmon coloured gown, with a white shrug and a single orange lily in her hair.

'She's not wearing jewellery,' said Herbert.

'He's taken her clutch!' gasped Annie.

'Straight into the inside pocket. Wow, he's quick,' said Aldemus.

'How did no one at the table notice?' asked Annie.

'Violet saw. She's watching him. Choosing to ignore him. Look,' said Louisa.

'Hmm. This isn't good. We shouldn't be here,' said Herbert.

'Yes. Something is very wrong,' said Louisa.

'Let's go. Leave now,' said Herbert and stood up.

'Yes. Let's,' said Annie and she jumped up to join him.

'I'm staying,' said Aldemus.

'So am I,' said Louisa.

Annie slowly sat back down.

'No, no, no. Let's go,' insisted Herbert but then stood in the doorway unsure of which way to turn.

IN THE GREAT hall where dinner was being served Frederick Cavanagan was up and down, moving all around the room and then vanishing again. Fifer observed this and the magic four closely. Fred made brief appearances leaving behind him a frequently empty chair. The Drake children were nowhere to be seen. Her suspicion increased.

'They know,' Fifer said softly to Nathan.

'It doesn't matter,' he replied.

'Someone has betrayed me,' said Fifer.

'It won't change things.'

Courses were short and sumptuous and the seating arrangement in constant flux, with people stopping to land like birds then flitting off again. Fred was back. Fifer was watching and counting the moving spectacle of gowns and tuxedos. She noted that Jackavoli and Penhaligon were the only guests absent from the room when Fred returned. So she watched the doors carefully. Penhaligon reappeared and took a seat at the table. Jackavoli's hat was balanced on the back of a chair, but there was still no sign of him. Fifer glared in direction of the hat, as the realisation dawned that Fred and Jackavoli were never in the room at the same time.

'I don't like this,' said Fifer.

'The Scion will triumph,' replied Nathan.

When the next course appeared, Fred ate quickly and again went to leave the room.

'It's Jackavoli. I think he's Frederick Cavanagan,' said Fifer standing up.

She followed him, watched him leave the room, but could not get to the door in time to see which direction he had taken. She stood in the doorway looking left and right down the long corridor, which was empty in both directions. She stepped into the corridor, closed the doors behind her and positioned herself out of sight on the gallery staircase, just past the great hall. She waited.

Eventually, the sound of whistling and footsteps came down the corridor towards her. She looked down the stairs and saw Jackavoli smoothing his hair. He was about to re-enter the hall.

'Fred!' she called, her voice a perfect mimic of Violet.

Jackavoli let his hands fall to his sides, stood still and did not enter the room.

'Fred, you've forgotten something,' Fifer said in Violet's tones and intonation.

He turned slowly and looked up the stairwell to find Fifer perched hawk-like at the top, brown eyes bearing down on him.

'Your name,' she said in her own voice.

'Is Jackavoli,' he replied, his voice light, his smile breaking wide, 'you sounded just like Violet Cavanagan. Fifer what are you doing? Is everything ok?'

She studied his face intently, but he was not nervous. She was no longer certain of his deception. She tapped her foot repeatedly in irritation. It was the only sound as they looked at each other. She could not afford to make a mistake. As if in response to the agitated tapping the Stone-carved poetry spell awoke. Silently the word 'Beware' appeared beautifully carved on the stone riser of the step for Fred to read. The word then appeared on the step below and the one below that.

'Where've you been?' she snapped.

'To walk my route, go over our plan.'

She stared at him, searching his face for signs of fear and saw only mild confusion. His body language was open; he kept his gaze lifted, let her look at him, waiting for her next move. The silence between them was thick and alive with energy. He wore an amicable smile and she an interrogative glare as they each contemplated killing the other, silently assessing the impact of such a disruption on their greater plans.

There was a creak, then the sound of a wooden door flung open, its handle banged against the stone. Not the entrance to the hall, but the gallery door. Herbert Cavanagan came cautiously out, saw Jackavoli and Fifer, kept his eyes down, descended the steps and ran quickly along the corridor to exit the castle. The briefest glimpse of shock, perhaps horror, registered on his father's face, in a micro-moment, involuntarily. Fifer's eyes had not moved. It was all she needed. She pushed her hand forward. There was a flash of blue light, a snare drum flick. The electric blow touched

Fred's heart, killing him instantly. He crumpled slowly to the floor.

The handles to the great hall moved. Someone was trying to open the doors. Fred's body lay in the way. Fifer flicked her wrist. Within seconds she had cremated him to a fine ash. The ash flew up, creating a swirling snow-globe outline of his fallen body, then disintegrated further. The guest tried the doors again and found no resistance. In the corridor all that remained of Frederick Cavanagan, was a light humidity that would soon vanish and a few flakes of white, which landed softly, as tiny specks on Nathan's tuxedo as he pushed open the doors.

Turning to him with a satisfied smile Fifer said,
'Now.'

THE MAGIC THREE

*N*athan looked at Fifer, nodded and straightened his jacket. They strode in opposite directions around the hall, indicating subtly and surely to anyone standing or about to rise that it was time for them to take their positions. Fifer returned to her seat. Nathan returned to his place at the table but remained standing. As soon as he did, chatter ceased, guests parted, the restless flittering about stopped. Violet and Esther sat calmly down, Violet feeling deeply uneasy. Horatio, already seated, filled his glass. There were two empty places at the table, no Jackavoli and no Fred. The three of the remaining magic four noticed and looked at each other in acknowledgement of the fact. Nathan took his glass, stepped on to his chair and then the table and walked confidently along it.

'And so I return, here, to the birthplace of magic, the hallowed ground of Raffaello Riviera, to the generous devotion of our kind hosts, to the place where I grew in knowledge and desolation... The perils of magic, the perils of the heart, the open heart...Horatio, Esther, Violet, magicians of our time, we all know there can only be one winner. I have already lost…everything I ever cared for, but I am here to claim my title, my territory, and my right to exist in Raffaello's footsteps. This is the path I am destined to tread.' He looked to Violet, Esther and finally Horatio with burning amber eyes; eyes that showed he was both broken and fearless. 'Let's begin.'

THE HARLESHAMP BAND brought the song to a close. Looking down at the band from the gallery Louisa noted a faint discordant hum coming from the stage. As she tried to place it, she saw the musician's relaxed stance vanish. Their movements were suddenly fast and synchronised. A violin bow was raised unusually high, held vertically. The guitarists lifted their instruments, rested the bases against their shoulders, and held them, heads pointing forwards, in a rifle position. Louisa watched, startled. The light reflected in a sharp glare from the raised violin bow and it seemed different now, like polished metal. Something was happening, Louisa saw, and she realised with a clench of fear that the magic four were all positioned with their backs to the stage. The drummer raised his sticks and crossed them above his head, as thin chains emerged from the tips, with sea urchin like attachments. The double base cracked down the middle like a door about to open. And the humming grew louder.

There was no time to speak. Louisa held her arms forward, her fingers splayed. Her magic flew towards the musicians in a fleeting silver arc. She caught them, seconds into their transformation and turned them into ice. Ice statues, one with a sabre held aloft, two with cross-bows poised to fire and the drummer with two flails crossed above his head. They twinkled under the lights, their faces contorted by their battle cries that had never reached sound. The black and gold rings of the deadly humming wasps could be seen in the now transparent body of the double base, slamming against the ice casing that would eventually kill them with their own poison.

Fifer had walked authoritatively to the doors of the great hall. She glanced at the musicians, her displeasure momentarily discernible. Then regathering her focus she addressed the room. Violet felt a sickness in her stomach and the sinking feeling, that she had been trying to dismiss, grew stronger as she looked at Fifer. What have you done? Violet thought, and as soon as she thought it, terror filled her heart as if to answer. Her heart beat loudly and the shock hit her like cold water. Her hands began to shake. She sensed what Fifer had done before Fifer spoke.

'Friends of the magic three, you are free to leave.' Fifer's soft voice projected to fill the room and was met with silence. Violet gasped and gripped the base of her chair tightly with both hands to steady herself. Esther closed her eyes momentarily. Horatio did not take his glare from Fifer, who flung open the doors open, 'Go, you may seek safety now!' No one moved. 'Anyone?' she asked, facing the room. She opened her arms and smiled. Something dark flew to her left arm and circled it at speed. A bracelet of onyx stones, set in gold, coiled around her bare arm like a glistening black snake. 'Then you must all be in allegiance with Nathan Glass.' Everyone stood, as if to attention, except Violet, Esther and Horatio. They watched as black velvet armbands with gold edging appeared on tuxedo sleeves, as gold cuff bracelets with black centres encircled delicate feminine arms and as a new tattoo appeared on the bicep of Sisco the sword swallower. Arm bands that signalled allegiance not to the magic four or their work, but to their death. Violet, Esther and Horatio looked into the eyes of the people around them, many of whom would not meet their gaze. None of the magic four had expected a full house.

From the gallery the three Drake children looked on in speechless bewilderment. Louisa and Aldemus were stunned by all Fifer had said. Annie who had avoided listening carefully, sat fearful and uncomprehending between her brother and sister. They held her hands, their eyes still fixed below, as a chill ran through them, the knowledge that Fred had probably been killed.

'Loyal or terrified?' came a strong gravelly voice from below and Marley Jaker walked into view of both Fifer and Nathan, but turned towards Nathan, looking up at him with open arms and questioning eyes. 'I'll respect you as the Scion; follow you as leader, if you let the truly terrified go. Loyalty through fear or respect Nathan, which do you want?'

'How touching, coming from a pirate,' spat Fifer.

'I want what is rightfully mine, my place in the history of magic,' said Nathan.

Marley nodded as if he understood.

'Don't!' snapped Fifer, glaring at Nathan.

He ignored her. 'Take them with you. You can leave now.'

Marley gave a small bow, gestured to the door and a third of the guests ran towards it. He waited until the last had exited and then swept out behind them. Fifer picked up the bracelets that fell in their rush and added them to her own arm. Suddenly Periwinkle Penhaligon turned, as if to follow the others. She placed her hand on his chest gently to block him.

'You're staying,' she whispered through a beautiful smile that froze him.

Soon the sounds of the fleeing footsteps faded. The guests who were left moved quickly, purposefully, in packs, to surround each of the remaining magic four. As they moved towards Violet she recognised some of the faces, from the list that Fred had given as his, under Jackavoli's command. With no one seemingly in authority, the group did not settle into position easily. Some stepped forward with initial courage then hesitated and fell back. Eventually a young man charged towards Violet in a burst of nervous aggression and grabbed her upper arm. He tried to force her to stand up. Glass and tableware smashed to the floor as he did so. Her arm did not move, despite his violence. She looked up at his face, at his eyes so full of the hunger for destruction. Calmly she felt her grief pushed to anger, the fire rising inside her. The room was quiet except for footsteps and the chinks of delicate broken glass falling. Then a gentler sound arose, like the roar of a small flame, and a crackle. Violet's assailant did not feel the pain at first. Then he looked down at his hand and ran away screaming. The fingers that had accosted her were reduced to stubs, burnt down to the first knuckle. She poured herself another drink.

Those who had earlier moved forward to encircle Violet had now stepped back, standing in a looser circle, with less certainty. Violet finished her drink and stood up. Then with the clip of heeled shoes running, a woman dived forward, outstretching the pendant from her necklace towards Violet. It was a silver disc set with coloured stones on a long chain. Violet recognised her face; it was someone she had taught to mix potions in the courtyard one crisp autumn morning. They had talked about their children, both had only children, boys. She had been quite good at mixing, Violet recalled, but under-confident, which must be why she relied on other people's magic now, through precious stones.

Violet looked closely at the pendant and noticed that one of the gem settings had been prized open roughly and was empty. Her eyes lit up for a second in satisfaction. 'He's got it!' she thought. Her suspicion was correct; the missing opal was indeed rolling around somewhere in Marley's trouser pocket. The woman noted with intense trepidation the look that had flashed across Violet's face.

'So careless,' Violet said, looking into the woman's eyes, then watched her as the seconds passed and nothing happened. The woman's lips and outstretched arm began to quiver. She looked at the pendant, saw the space where the opal should have been, gulped for air and looked pleadingly at those who stood around her. They looked away. The necklace began to tighten and its rope chain shortened, as the disc drew slowly up to the middle of her chest.

'No, no! Please, no!' she cried.

'How's your son? Similar age to Herbert, isn't he?' asked Violet.

The woman was perspiring, her face as wet and shiny as the Harleshamp ice statues.

'Yes,' she replied, so quietly, it was almost a mime.

The necklace shortened again, the pendant jumping up to the height of her collarbones. The woman grabbed the chain with both fists and tried to bring it down. It shot up, out of her hands, forming a choker. The disc swung slightly.

'Yes,' Violet replied and walked away. The necklace tightened, like firm hands around the woman's throat and others rushed to help tear it from her neck.

The net of people surrounding Violet loosened, but did not dissolve completely as she strode out of the hall. Several made as if to follow her and collided in their hurry, then broke into a run to keep up with her. She led them deliberately to the East Wing, the opposite point from where they were intended to be. Lady Dukes and Nicholas Rumpkin broke from their positions to follow at the back of the group pursuing Violet.

OUTSIDE THE CASTLE, in the cold night air, Marley walked up and down. His long dark hair was tossed around by the wind; a lengthy silver scar became visible on his neck. He had a manic and disturbed energy as he paced, like a caged tiger. Through growling commands he got the guests to line up in rows on the castle steps. He stood before them so that he could see each face and look directly into their eyes. His eyes were intense and fearsome. The guest shivered, in the bitter breeze and apprehension.

He opened his arms wide, his palms facing towards them. He smiled, revealing two sharp, pewter-coloured teeth in amongst the ivory. The guests' eyes widened before they felt warmth flood their bodies and their muscles immediately relaxing. Marley's arms remained wide as all their concerns dissolved. Many sat down or reclined on the stone, without feeling its icy bite. Sleepy, yet attentive the audience propped up their heads and listened.

'Now I have little speech for you, which you'll take away with you. First let's get all your minds aligned.' He looked in to each individual's eyes and thus briefly their thoughts. 'That's it, good. So, it's due to the gracious kindness of the Drakes and Cavanagans that you're alive. Never forget that. You'll have no recollection of your part in this treacherous plot. Undeservingly, you'll be freed from your guilt, shame and cowardice. Small mercies. You will remember my face.' For a second he dropped his arms to his sides and gave them his most menacing expression. They jolted back in alarm and he quickly returned his arms and their mood. 'You will fear me, Marley Jaker, for supporting Nathan Glass in trying to destroy the two greatest magic families this island has ever seen. And you will hand me all of your jewellery before you make your way home. You can leave now.'

Compliantly they all stood; relaxed and comfortable they handed over their sparkling jewels, golden trinkets and finery. Marley filled his pockets as they made their way into the forest.

. . .

In the Great Hall, Nathan, standing on the table, turned to face Horatio, who sat smiling defiantly at him from his throne-like seat at the end. Nathan's feet were firmly planted, his arms folded across his chest as he looked directly at his rival. Horatio looked up at him briefly, helped himself to a petit four and bit into it, dark chocolate coating a lump of sweetened ginger. He put it immediately back down. Why would a chocolatier do that? The ratio of ginger to dark chocolate should only ever be around 25:75 at the most. He would need to speak to the chef, get more samples before the next party. He looked for something to take the taste away.

Nathan walked towards him. Horatio continued to drink from a delicate coffee cup, to quench the taste of ginger reverberating in his mouth. He eventually looked up, after a few moments, to meet Nathan's waiting eyes.

'Shall we retire to the battlement roof? The view is so much better from there,' said Nathan.

'Certainly,' replied Horatio, placing down his coffee cup.

Horatio stretched his arms and then interlaced his fingers behind his head. He exhaled with along, melodramatic sigh of intense boredom aimed directly at Nathan. Undetected, the gust of air grew in force as it shot through Nathan's legs. He felt it as a cold shiver around his calves before it rose like a wave behind him and slammed him face first on to the table. Crockery and glassware shattered as Nathan landed, narrowly missing Horatio's unmoved cup and saucer. Nathan looked up, wine running down his face. Horatio shook his head and smiled.

'Always was such a bad sport,' Horatio sighed. And with that, he completely disappeared.

ESTHER'S GUESTS

*E*sther stood up, her gold dress glimmering and bright. Several people at the table also stood immediately, including the man to her right, with whom she had been speaking convivially for the early part of the evening. She looked closely at those gathered around her, allocated to her downfall and sat back down on her chair. Confused, they looked to each other then all sat back down. She placed her hand gently on the upper arm of the man to her right, and felt the velvet armband, soft to the touch. This was Francis Birch, known to all as Birch. He was minor magic, from a once distinguished but rapidly declining magic family line. He was built like a lumberjack and had a naturally pouting mouth, which seemed to signal permanent displeasure.

'Now, where were we, before the interruption?' she asked, her eyes honest and open. 'We were getting along so well.'

His lips pressed together in discomfort and his brow furrowed in annoyance. 'Ah, I see. I'm not supposed to speak. Would that make it easier for you? To turn on the switch of hate without having to face the fact that I am real? Destroy the magic four, stand by Nathan, but I live and breathe next to you. I enjoy the salmon mousse, am warmed by the cassoulet spices and delight in the taste of the wine, just as you do. Make decisions about my future based on what I feel is just and right, as you do. Yet you would see the light in me go out. To decide is one thing, the act of destroying me another. Are you ready to see me take my last breath? To kill me? Because it seems that the time is now. No, don't look to them; you're the one closest to me. They're looking to you for action.'

Birch did not need her to confirm this; he could feel their eyes on him. He looked at his plate, his shoulders tense, his face flushed. 'Have you been set up? That must feel awful. Or were you hoping to escort me out of this room, to lead me to my destruction elsewhere? Is that what you would like? Then take my hand.'

She offered her hand, her yellow sapphire ring sparkling under the light. She smiled. Feeling hot, he tugged at the neck of his shirt, took her hand clumsily in his sweaty grasp and they stood up. The others at the table stood as before.

Fifer Savine began to make her way towards them from across the room. Birch waited for Esther to move, his hand moist as he held hers. She stood looking at him, 'You lead,' she said quietly and he walked her towards the door, more as if he were leading her on to a dance floor than to her death. She felt magic hitting her back, cold like rain and dagger-sharp, but she had prepared for that; everything they threw at her was deflected back into the room. Those relying on jewellery charged by Nathan and Fifer, without the skill to return or neutralise the ricocheting magic, came off worst from their own wicked intent. Several fell to the floor and never rose again. The skilled jumped to action, quick enough to cancel out their own work. Fifer came closer.

Birch led Esther out of the great hall and the large doors immediately closed behind them. He looked anxiously over his shoulder. He heard and felt the attempts to force the doors open from inside, but they stayed firm. Esther smiled. The lights went out. The corridor was in complete darkness.

'I'll lead now,' said Esther, 'keep hold of my hand and you'll be fine.'

Esther walked down the dark corridor in the opposite direction that Violet had taken. He held tight as she picked up pace. His feet stumbled in a half run. She gained in speed. She was stronger than he expected. She ran, dragging him along. He had no idea where in the castle he was when she came to an abrupt stop. He could not see her. She pulled her hand away from his grasp. The footfalls, her breathing, the movement of her gown, all the sounds of her presence vanished. Silence.

Then music: a music box, playing something he recognised, in plucked, mechanical sound. The lights came on. He was staring down a long corridor. All doors leading from it were closed. The music came from the room closest to him. He saw Esther at the very end, in the far distance. Her laughter sounded close behind him, he jumped and turned and there she was at the other end in the distance, her back to him. The laughter sounded again, close, as if she were right by his ear. He turned startled and looked directly into her eyes, yet the image of her in the background was still there. He felt a cool hand on his shoulder from behind, he turned again, to be in close range with her piercing grey eyes and yet still another image of her in the distance. The laughter tinkled like notes of pure sound and surrounded him.

'Four Esthers,' he said in amazement.

'Your charming dinner companion was the real one,' said the Esther he happened to be staring at.

The door nearest to him opened and he could see the music box open on a small table.

'But there is no time to play games,' said another Esther over his shoulder. Then both of them were behind him, pushing him forward with incredible force, into the room. The door slammed and with its closure the brass handle became a deadlock, the wood turned to metal and a glass square appeared in the top centre panel. 'Make yourself at home dear friend.'

Noise filled the castle, as the doors to the great hall were forced open. One Esther stood close to the corner that they would have to turn to reach the corridor. Black tuxedos and the dark pink of Fifer Savine stormed into view. The nearest Esther was pushed and fell to the ground. They cried out in anger as they gathered around her. Fifer sent an electric blow to the heart and her body shuddered with eyes closed. Everyone waited. As the silence grew, a second Esther joined the crowd peering down at her own lifeless body.

'I don't think she's dead,' she said, smiling with wicked eyes, waiting for Fifer's gaze to meet hers. When their eyes met Fifer's filled with shock and fear. The two remaining Esthers appeared behind Fifer, grabbed her under each arm, and pulled her backwards to a doorway, which opened behind her.

The Esther, once suspected dead, had now risen from the floor. She smiled and used the lightest of touches to send Fifer reeling backwards into the morning room where she crashed to the floor. Four ghostly Esthers stood in the doorway, merging and unmerging into one solid form. Before Fifer could recover, the door that had opened in solid wood slammed closed in heavy metal. It had become a prison cell door. Fifer's anguished face soon stared through the glass square, her hammering fists unheard, all sound swallowed by the weight of the door.

Without Fifer the group became nervous, hesitant, edged away from the cluster of Esthers or clung desperately to each other and looked around for a way to escape. Some attacked, but all were confronted by a glowing Esther who blew out their spells like party candles and carefully redirected their path. The flashes of magic retaliation eventually stopped. The only sounds were of fast shallow breath and involuntary murmurs of panic. The guests were grouped in twos or threes not daring to move. All four Esthers looked at them, then at each other and seemed to reach a decision.

They paced the corridor like restless lionesses. The guests automatically stepped back closer to the walls. More doorways appeared in the stone and the doors opened silently. Those caught off balance fell into the rooms, those able to steady themselves watched and waited. There were two Esthers at either end of the corridor. Simultaneously they sprinted towards each other. Soundless and ghost-like they collided, transforming back into one solid Esther who now looked at them in fury.

'In,' she commanded.

Heads hanging in shame and embarrassment they stepped inside the rooms without resistance.

'Welcome to my home. Stay I insist, at my pleasure.'

Esther walked past the open doors, head held high and said: 'I simply won't hear of you leaving.' Then the sound of metal doors slamming echoed like waves of thunder around the castle.

VIOLET'S ROOKS

The great hall was empty except for Nathan Glass and the Drake children watching him from the gallery. He had cleaned himself up and sat on the middle of the table hugging his knees. He did not look powerful. Aldemus and Louisa both wondered if he could really be the Scion. Shards of broken glass still entangled in his hair threw back the light from the icicle chandelier under which he sat. It looked as if its tendrils had dripped diamonds onto him. Red wine had stained one side of his shirt and his collar was marked with gravy. He jumped down from the table, straightened his jacket and collar and strode out of the room.

Nathan walked the path Esther had taken, not long after she had left it. All was quiet now. He glanced at the small square windows in the newly created doors. Through one he caught the eye of Fifer Savine, but he kept on walking.

ON THE OTHER side of the castle Violet stood with her back against the wall, raising herself to full height, adrenalin firing through her body. She forced herself to remain calm, to use it to think quickly. Whippet thoughts darted through her mind, picking up others as they ran. The crowd were advancing towards her, as if in slow motion. There were many more than they had planned for and they were all baying for blood.

The new leaders parted the crowd as they came forward; a gleam from the rose-gold pocket watch of Rumpkin and a shimmer from the rooster-feathered hat of Lady Dukes. Predators gaining ground, the bold ones letting the nervous exist in the protection of their shadow. Violet stretched out her arms against the wall behind her, feeling the texture of the stone. The traitors grew in number and confidence. The numbers mattered. It made them brave enough to take her down. United together, they advanced.

Violet anticipated and deflected attacks from the crowd in the foreground. Most were amateurish, but some smarted nevertheless, as she made space behind her defences for the greater spell she was creating. Her mind and her magic were focused; she was nearly there, but not quite ready. She had to stall them; delay them to gain time.

Rumpkin sent out stronger magic, something darker that felt like needle scratches down her face and neck. She was able to stop whatever evil it was before it injected in and took hold. In lightning-speed retaliation, from her hands, a fiery white light shot out with a whoosh of water-cascading sound. They all slid uncontrollably, bones thwacking against the ground, which was turning to ice. Rumpkin and Dukes recovered fast and held firm as the other guests tumbled like dominos on either side of them. In her mind Violet could see the sky and the entrance she had once made to another world, cut through like a knife, her greatest spell to date.

'Out! Out!' she cried, her voice projecting and echoing down the corridor. Light surrounded her. The irises of her eyes flashed to silver, then darkened to indigo. Her gaze punched into their chest. Gasps, wheezes, coughs, throats spluttered, people collapsed. Hearts lurched, the force driving them back metres. The ice beneath transformed to vapour; the air became damp. Evaporation rose with a low siren hum as her spell filled the vast space and resounded.

'Out!' she cried again. The castle wall to her left began to crumble, brick by brick falling in silent avalanche as the siren sound increased in volume.

The night air raced in and whipped up around the traitors. The pain in their chests pulled them upwards, impaled like fish, flapping, floundering. A ruby ring, a silk handkerchief, a golden cuff, opulence falling like rain to the ground as they ascended. Once above the castle Rumpkin smiled and vanished. Dukes struggled, freed herself and flew in falcon form into the night. Violet watched their escape, counting. Losses were expected, but not desired. There would be time to return. She had gathered 29 people.

'Out, Out!' She yelled into the night. Those in the sky, shrouded in evaporation, moved as fast as her whippet thoughts could direct them. Shooting, firing, faster than stars, over the dark forest and hills, past the town and beyond, to the northern forest they flew. There they came to an abrupt stop. They hung above the trees, suspended in a moment of dread, before they plunged down, down to the Waiting Room door, which was open and ready. 'Out!' No waiting. Like forward fire, from artillery, they went shooting through. The siren sound receded. All 29 were out. Lurching onto the wet grass of a London park, Axel field, 29 rooks appeared. The door between worlds slammed shut. No return; cast out. 29 rooks cawed and screeched, jumped with wings outstretched and bent, pecked at each other, and frantically searched for a doorway back. A doorway that they would never find, now their magic had been taken from them.

Violet slid down the castle wall to the floor, her knees

bent, her head in her hands, the edges of her emerald gown wet, looking black from the pools of thawing ice that surrounded her. She tapped her fingers against the ground. The bricks responded to the sound and rhythm and clambered quickly back up into their rightful places. Soon the wall was strong again, the damp air the only evidence of her trouble. She stood up carefully, turned her feet resolutely and headed to the battlement roof.

IN THE DARKNESS all of the figments happened to arrive on the dance floor at the same time. Betty wandered in, with an empty bottle of whiskey. The artist fell through an unlocked door, spilling more paint. Katy Cavelle was in there already, sort of smiling, which caused immediate concern for everyone. It was when she offered to help the artist up from the floor, when all the figments realised that she was being nice, that everyone in the darkness became truly terrified. They froze and stared at her. She froze too with that eerie, difficult smile still on. She gently examined her lips with her fingers. The Firebrand let out a low rumble and the door handle of the flame room shook. The Firebrand could smell fear, Nathan's. It kicked open the flame room door, leaving a black footprint singed onto it.

Katy paced up and down. The Firebrand approached her, lighting up the dark corners of the vast space, flicking its tail erratically. Katy's piercing green eyes opened wide. The room they bustled through every day now appeared completely unfamiliar. Her lipstick had smudged up to her nostrils and she looked as if she had been punched in the face. She and the Firebrand looked at each other, their faces creased in confusion and concern, neither comforted by the other's presence.

The artist's overalls looked like a butcher's. The artist

stared at the Firebrand intensely and made it feel uncomfortable. The Firebrand closed its eyes and breathed deeply, lungs expanding to make the space feel suffocating. Betty alternated between, throwing her arms up and shouting obscene comments, then apologising and asking for whiskey. The artist cursed in German and Italian, which he had never learned or spoken before. The Firebrand's tail smacked nervously against the floor and occasionally undulated upwards to crack like a whip. The sound made the figments jump and gasp. The Firebrand twitched, its eyes stricken yellow flames. Nathan Glass was scared and it could not rest.

THE BATTLEMENTS

*N*athan reached the battlement roof first. Horatio had not yet materialised; so Nathan stood in the exact spot that he guessed Horatio planned to appear. Although he took his time, when Horatio did appear, he was wrong footed, he lost his balance, banged into Nathan and was forced to take a step backwards. Horatio's alert eyes stared at the face of his enemy and drank in the features he had once so admired. He saw how Nathan had aged, became aware of how much time had passed.

'She chose the better man,' Horatio said eventually, his voice projecting louder than it needed to.

'You don't actually believe that,' replied Nathan.

Horatio's forehead creased, his features darkening in the exact same way that Nathan remembered from years ago. His agitation impossible to mask, a light retort no longer an option, his anger rising.

'You were in love with her. That's why you are here, because she chose me and in your naivety you thought she could love you. Jealousy is destructive. Who cares if you are the Scion? Certainly not Esther. It might help you form an army, if you want to take out the competition, but let's not pretend that's why you're here. You had no interest in the castle or in power even. Unrequited love has deformed you. Scion or not, and we will find out, you are weak.'

'Unrequited love,' said Nathan calmly, looking into Horatio's eyes. 'What do you know of that Horatio? Of how it feels, to desire what you cannot have?'

Horatio froze, waited for him to continue. 'I think you know. Esther should too, because she has your hand, but she has never had your heart, that's far too closely guarded.'

'You sound so sure,' said Horatio.

'We make our own prisons. Nothing is so hollow, so empty as a life unlived.'

Horatio, stunned, stared at him hard and did not speak. 'Just space for poetry to echo around,' Nathan finished. Horatio eyes darkened into resolve and he smiled as if mildly amused.

'You speculate wildly. There is victory. There is always victory. Let's both go for that,' he said finally. Then he vanished, leaving Nathan alone at the top of the castle.

NICHOLAS RUMPKIN APPEARED in the ground floor corridor. Immediately his manic eyes glinted in alarm. He sensed that something was before him that he could not see. His mind processed that there were three people advancing towards him, but he was not quite quick enough. Aldemus's invisible fingertips circled his neck. Nicholas lost his footing and his equilibrium as he was dragged backwards to an open doorway. Annabelle and Louisa pushed him inside. Slam. When Lady Dukes appeared around the corner they ran to her, the three Drake children mustering all their powers to send her back. Aldemus was fast and her magic could not counter his speed. The force of the attack sent her reeling to the floor.

With their hearts pounding, jubilant and adrenalin fuelled, the three Drake children held hands and walked determinedly, to cover the width of the corridor, so no remaining traitors could escape their net. The castle was quiet, the great hall empty; all guests were imprisoned or gone. Salem appeared in his tuxedo sweeping with a broom and walked closest to Annie who blocked his path and watched his face wrinkle in confusion. Aldemus let out a nervous laugh. When Salem's face instantly showed fear Louisa switched them back to visible. They expected him to be surprised, then stern, but eventually to smile at their audacity; instead he just looked horrified.

'You must go. You should not be here!' he said.

'Where've you been? Weren't you at dinner?' asked Aldemus.

'I saw Nathan arrive. I took mine in the courtyard.'

'Where are mum and dad?' asked Annie.

'You have to go,' said Salem, putting his arms around them and trying to physically move them along.

'No,' said Louisa.

'They need our help,' said Aldemus.

'They do not want you here. It is not part of their plan!'

'Nor was the death of Frederick Cavanagan,' said Louisa.

'What?' said Annie.

'You have to go,' said Salem.

'Fred? Not Fred!' said Annie.

'Where is Nathan Glass?' asked Aldemus.

'No,' said Salem shaking his head, 'Go!'

'After you, Salem,' said Louisa gesturing to the way out.

Salem looked away and shook his head in despair.

'To the bitter end,' said Aldemus.

'Four Drakes are stronger than two,' snapped Louisa.

'And Annie can play the violin,' said Aldemus. Annie wasn't listening. She was looking out of the window.

'Frederick Cavanagan's not dead! Look he is up there. That must be Fred on the battlement roof. There is someone there, see!'

'No. That's Nathan Glass,' said Louisa. She looked eagerly at Aldemus. 'If we stay in the shadows we will be undetected.'

'Let's go. Annie stay with Salem,' said Aldemus.

Annie did as she was told, lost for words, sinking into sadness. The fight in her knocked out by the news of Fred's death. Louisa and Aldemus walked the corridors to the darkest part of the courtyard and glided ghost-like and silent out into the cold air. Annie and Salem peered cautiously out of the window. In the sky above, something like a star was glowing brightly. They noticed, but paid it little attention.

Then, before they could move, lights went up outside, like flares firing from three sides of the battlement roof. Green, gold and red, as Violet, Esther and Horatio appeared, illuminating the face of Nathan Glass who stood on the fourth side.

At once the light surrounding the magic three began to dim as they faced Nathan.

'He's going to kill them! He's going to kill them!' screamed Annie, tears running down her face.

'No. They'll destroy him,' said Salem, patting her shoulder.

'He's going to kill them! He's going to kill them!' screamed Annie. She leant forward against the window ledge hyperventilating.

'They're attacking him now; he is faltering. Horatio's light is growing stronger.'

'He is destroying them. Violet is flickering! All of her is flickering! She is going to burn out!'

Salem continued to pat her shoulder. His heart sinking, he checked his watch and grimaced.

'This is when I am supposed to leave the castle. They gave

clear instructions. You're not even supposed to be here! Let's get Aldemus and Louisa back and go.'

'No! Stay with me! Stay here!' she shrieked.

Salem gave a deep sigh and nervously ran his fingers through his hair.

'Then look at the comet, up there in the sky Annie; at least, it looks like a comet, see its tail. Focus on the comet.'

LOUISA CLOSED HER EYES. In her mind she tried to bring forth all the magic energy from within her. She concentrated her power and imagined sending it out like a laser beam directly to Violet; she clenched her fists, scrunched up her face and felt her energy leave in fierce acceleration. Violet's light grew brighter and her magic exploded like a roman candle, raising itself upwards.

'Keep safe. Keep safe. Please. Please,' muttered Salem quietly.

Aldemus concentrated on Nathan to weaken his magic, break its focus. The immediate resistance he felt from Nathan's power sent him flying backwards, smashing him against the stone wall, but still he fought. Together Louisa and Aldemus worked, concealed in the shadows, moving when necessary, avoiding the circles of light from the lanterns.

'SALEM, look in the sky. It's moving faster now, coming forward. Not a comet. Look at that speed. What is it?' said Annie.

THE WEB of spells to seal the castle had been carefully orchestrated and expertly sewn. Time could not be turned back.

The Firebrand roared, like a crack of thunder above them. In blinding light, it advanced downwards with a wild guttural cry that resonated through the castle and the people within its walls. Then it slowed and returned to its huge original form in the sky above them. The magic three knew they only had seconds left. The Firebrand illuminated the castle like daylight, as if it were the sun. It looked at Esther, its eyes wide, forcing her to shield her eyes. Then she looked down into the brightly lit courtyard.

THE MAGIC THREE were losing to Nathan. He had never needed Fifer's army to destroy them, just the confidence to be able to return and prove who he was. Violet was fading and fought back relentlessly, alight with anger, too late to save those she loved. In her exhaustion the awaiting grief found an inlet. Oh Fred. She felt herself slipping away into the night sky. She never wanted to burn out like this. The horror of what Nathan had done, the outrage brought her back. She summoned all the power within her, bigger and beyond her physical self and sent it out to destroy him. He must suffer. The stone walls reverberated with the force of her passion, the heartfelt desire for justice and for revenge. Nathan stood juddering, fists clenched, taking the blow. Her magic gone, all that was left of her was a floating sensation that would fade like warm breath into the cold night. The thought, her last thought, was that revenge did not taste sweet; it tasted of blood, through clenched teeth, rank and repulsive.

HORATIO'S RAGE was an iron claw, poised to hurt, disfigure, cut through to the bone. He stood strong and grounded. There would be physical evidence of his work. His power was a wild sea of hatred that he now channelled forward. He stood, his stature more imposing than ever, his glare unhinged and fixed. His eyes were met firmly and directly by Nathan's cold stare. This sent Horatio's magic screaming out at astounding speed. The ferocious power of Horatio's final charge took all that existed of Horatio. No time for thought; his fury, his end. Horatio burnt out and Nathan lay crumpled, injured.

ESTHER HAD SEEN the faces of her children in the courtyard. Her determined eyes widened and dissolved into terror. For a moment she could not breathe. Frozen, she felt sickness plummet through her whole body. Her Flourishes had been released, to rectify any disruption to the web of spells sealing the castle. She knew that they would prevent any way out. She staggered, her head spinning and attempted to hold the magic back. She could not. It was stronger than her. Her breath came now in loud, rapid gasps.

'Run!' she screamed at them.

They could not hear her. 'Run!" she yelled again and felt the back of her throat tearing. She appeared to them now as a blurred figure. The magic working against her, to block her out, for no one was to leave. They looked up at her squinting, uncomprehending. She ran screaming at them, hoping they would see her from a different vantage point. But she knew what was happening, she saw the patterns in her mind, she struggled to breathe, and she tried violently to break everything they had carefully constructed.

Nathan struggled up from the ground, sat dishevelled on the floor and watched her fighting the tide of magic she could not control. She stopped, tried again with everything that there was of her. But what stood before her was unassailable and what was left of her was weak and ailing. Crying, panting, she continued, she collapsed to the stone floor, pulled at the roots of her hair, howled wide-mouthed and shook her head wildly. She stood again, teetered, tried to find a way, fell hard onto the stone. She was aware of the magic locking and interlocking all around her, like doors closing and bolts sliding, all just out of reach. The sky above them was now lit with fire, the Firebrand hovering. Esther perspired in its heat, her hair sticking to her face. She looked down into the courtyard, still refusing to fall to the exhaustion that was trying to claim her. The view below became completely obscured from above; just as the magic four had once so meticulously planned, as they had sat thoughtfully in their velvet chairs.

ESTHER LOOKED up at the descending sky of flames, and then around at the battlement roof, which was bathed in the Firebrand's orange light. No more Horatio. No more Violet. Her chest tightened, her heart pounded. She felt so unsteady that the ground seemed to be moving, when it was not. It was just she and Nathan left. He staggered across to her, battle scarred, yet composed, unaffected by the heat. They looked at each other uncertainly. Neither wished to show the other mercy, yet both were compelled to do so, to gain time; Nathan wondering if love could save him and Esther rapidly devising a new plan. His heart pounded as he held out his hand to help her up. Glaring at him she took it and stood next to him quivering. He looked up, said some soft reassuring words to the dragon, and then issued it a firm command.

The Firebrand arched its back and lowered its chin, letting out a disgruntled screech to show its displeasure as it began its retreat. Then Nathan made a wide sweeping motion with his arm, across where he and Esther were standing, as if he was slashing the air before them with a knife, while he whispered an almost silent spell. Then all went black as soot, then charcoal grey. Falling ash covered the roof and transformed through shades of grey until it became as white as snow, then disappeared entirely. It revealed clouds racing across a blue sky. It was morning and the battlement roof empty.

PART V

AFTER THE WINTER BALL

*H*erbert fled the winter ball, ran down the steps of the castle, sprinted into the forest and headed towards home. Panic increased inside him. He tried to run away from it, to out run the terrible feeling. He zipped through the dark southern forest, faster and faster. He hurdled fallen trees, jumped over brambles as he went. They could be in danger. They had wanted him to stay away. He needed to get back home. The deep sinking feeling flooded his body. He sped up. It was just this forest, this awful place, he hoped. He let out a loud cry of frustration as he ran and startled the nocturnal creatures.

Something deep inside terrified him. A fear so engulfing he could not let it rise, he resisted it, ran. It waited. He became tired, his heart pounded, his breath was ragged. As his worst fears entered his mind their voices came. In his head or in the forest, he could not be sure.

'Herbert, it will be ok. We love you,' said Fred.

'We love you. This is not what we planned,' said Violet.

He had felt the tremors emanating from the castle,

someone had burned out, maybe more. He did not want to think about that. He ran faster. He tried and failed to gather his thoughts as he went, enough to use his magic to get him there quicker. He found that he could not focus, he could only run, through the forest, the country lanes, the town, the fields to the edge of the northern forest, that felt like home. He slowed for breath.

When he finally arrived in the clearing before Cavanagans, he saw that the door to Cavanagans was open. Millicent had returned home on her broomstick long before. The fire was out; embers were left, with specks glowing orange in the charcoal. His breathing levelled out as he walked to the door. He heard an owl hoot close by and looked up at the trees, but could not see it. When he looked back his parents were standing by the fire. They turned to look at him, pleased to see him. He was surprised to see them and sighed with relief.

'Oh, thank goodness for that. I was so worried.'

He walked over to them, to hug them. Fred's smile softened and he looked serious.

'Sit down Herb,' he said, before Herbert could reach him.

Herbert collapsed onto the sofa exhausted.

'I'm so glad you're here,' Herbert said as he lay back.

'You are the best son anyone could ever have,' Fred said and smiled, his eyes welling up. Herbert sat up.

'And you have made us happier than you will ever know. Our joy. You have been our joy from the moment you arrived,' said Violet looking intently at him, also smiling and holding back tears.

'You are an amazing boy. Kind, brave, strong, funny, a shining light that we love to be around,' said Fred.

They looked at him affectionately. The kind words stoked his feelings of terror. He stood up, his voice filled with desperation,

'No! No! This is a spell!'

Tears ran down Violet's face and she nodded.

'No! This is a spell triggered by your deaths!' He kicked over a table.

'We wanted to say goodbye. It is time to say goodbye. I'm so sorry,' said Fred and their images began to fade.

'No! No!' screamed Herbert. He ran to them, to hold them, but they were not solid form. He stood as close to them as he could get, shaking, unable to breathe properly.

'We are in this room because we want you to know that you are loved, even though we are gone. We will love you your whole life long Herbert Cavanagan,' said Violet. Their images flickered, faded and vanished.

Herbert staggered to the wall, beat it with his hands. Then he stared into the embers of the fire and held on tightly to the mantelpiece. He choked on his tears, cried and cried. He did not see the words come. Slowly carving appeared in the stone centre of the fireplace. Weakly the tired spell of Horatio worked its magic, errant and faltering, yet boldly it wrote: 'what will remain of us is love'.

As NATHAN and Esther travelled towards the darkness he drifted in and out of consciousness. His skin was sickly white; each breath was a painful shudder and return, his rib cage sore and aching. In his disorientated state he thought his back heart was visible to the world. That it could be seen through the veil of pale skin, contained in its bone-cage, beating, pumping and jet-black, like the tip of a burnt match held in white molten wax.

They arrived and his legs gave way; he collapsed and fell hard onto the floor. He lay supine, feeling confused and remembered when he had lain next to Fred on the aquarium floor. Yes Fred you were right, this is what it feels like, just as we imagined. Well done Fred, well done Fred. So clever. Did I kill you? Horatio killed me. No, I killed Horatio. No. Where is the golden light, where is Esther?

Nathan opened his eyes and looked around at the familiar shapes of the reception in the darkness. Esther was standing nearby and he felt relief flood through him. He sat up. Immediately Katy Cavelle appeared and deftly pulled him up to stand. She spoke softly to him, to reassure him. Katy looked Esther up and down in judgement then walked away. He managed to balance and stay upright, to offer his arm to Esther and stagger forward through the darkness towards the contemplation room.

Betty was at her desk. She looked at him, stood up, her mouth open in disbelief, her eyes filling with tears.

'Say nothing,' Nathan said, in a feeble voice, without looking at her. He tried and struggled to open the contemplation room door, his hand suddenly rigid and immobile, slipping, unable to get a hold on the lock. 'Don't!' he cried out, feeling her desire to help, her good intentions. She did not move. He scraped around at the handle until he managed to open it, wincing in pain. He waited, held open the door and Betty turned to look at Esther, who followed him into the contemplation room. Betty opened the brown book and ticked Esther's name.

Nathan and Esther stood for a few moments looking out at the landscape.

'I can't believe you are here. It doesn't seem real,' Nathan said.

'It's real,' Esther replied calmly.

'For so long I imagined what it would be like, having you here. I want it to be perfect for you. I designed everything with you in mind, but if you don't like it I can change it, change anything, everything. You will stay, won't you?'

'Yes.'

She did not look at him, but took in the view of the canyon. The sunlight caught her hair and the breeze blew it from her face. Wincing in pain he began to gently beat his left thigh. The curses, bestowed upon him on the battlement roof, were kicking in.

'It feels like knives, just like knives,' he said.

'It probably is. I imagine that is what he would have wanted you to feel. Horatio is very much about the physical, I have no doubt that it is his work.'

'How do you know it is not Violet?' Nathan asked and managed a half smile as his discomfort started to subside and his pleasure at being in her company worked its way through.

'I know my husband.'

Nathan looked surprised. 'And no doubt the pain in your bones will be the worst. Eventually you'll anticipate it, a whole harmony of notes from sharp to low; he will have probably set it to Bach. If you work out which piece you will be able to see his vision. Not that it will make the pain any more tolerable, unless you take comfort in its certainty. His capacity for cruelty was always longing for an outlet. Your pain will be his symphony, his burn out, his greatest work.'

'I love you,' Nathan said.

'It is hard being here,' she said, turning to look at him. She was tired and impatient and trying to rein in both feelings. He felt the sharpness.

'Yes, of course, I'm sorry.'

'We were meant to be together,' she replied without emotion.

A broad smile lit Nathan's face and was followed immediately by an intense feeling of being stabbed in the side, which took his breath away.

'I need space, I need time, I need my own room,' she said.

'Everything you wish.'

'I'll create it myself. I'll have it here.'

She drew a doorway with her hand, opened the door, walked through and closed it. He staggered to his feet, walked to the door and with his finger traced her name on it. The letters appeared like gold fireworks and fizzed like the excitement within him. His eyes were smiling as the pain in his knee joints made him fall again to the floor.

IN THE CASTLE LIBRARY LOUISA stood, porcelain white, her dark hair dishevelled. A plum coloured bruise was forming on her face, from where she had been hit by a flailing fist of Nicholas Rumpkin. She stared at her red leather book resting on the desk. It had been useful; it had helped them separate and isolate all of the first order magicians. Aldemus had been relieved and grateful for her records. She had never intended her work to be used for such bleak and horrifying purpose. She glared at the book with hateful eyes.

Annie could not stop crying. She sat collapsed in a chair hanging her head. Her face was a swollen waterfall of tears, her gulps and gasps the only sound in the room. Aldemus paced up and down, treading lightly, but moving manically. His dark features set in deep creases of concern. Salem had led them there in silence and then left them, so that he could check the external doors, although he knew they were locked. He just needed to feel the metal of each one against his skin to be sure, for certainty, for precision and order. Between short breaths and tears Annie blurted,

'They'll be ok, they're safe, they'll rescue us! Won't they Aldemus? Won't they?'

She looked up. Aldemus did not look at her, but closed his eyes and sighed.

'We need to talk about how many burned out,' he said.

'What do you mean!' she shouted.

'He means how many on the battlements burned out trying to kill Nathan Glass and if Nathan burned out too,' said Louisa.

'But mum and dad and all of the magic four, except Fred were on the roof. They will be fine. They are the best magicians! No one burned out,' she said irritated. Then she sat up, composed herself and began tidying her hair.

'You didn't feel them then?' Aldemus asked her.

'Feel what?' she replied.

'The tremors, when a magician burns out,' he replied.

'No,' she replied in alarm, and then in anger, 'No!'

'Louisa, how many?' Aldemus asked.

'I don't know for certain if I'm right. The dragon's roar blurred things.'

'Two?' he asked.

'Two,' she replied solemnly.

'But Aldemus, not mum and dad! Not mum and dad!' Annie shouted.

Louisa sped from the room. Aldemus sank into a chair and held his head in his hands. Annie slowly stood, walked over and sat limply in the chair next to him, all colour drained from her face. He hugged her as she began to sob and through his own tears said,

'We don't know Annie, we don't know.'

She hugged him back, numb and lifeless.

Louisa stormed into the great hall, took the ornamental mace that had hung by the fireplace since the days of the Riviera family and walked the corridors of the castle. The sound of it banging against the first metal door was like a gunshot. Louisa spoke in a voice she hardly recognised, booming like her father, but with a harder edge. She used magic to allow her voice to be heard and to receive back answers. She walked, smashed the mace against specific doors and asked questions until she was satisfied and then returned them to soundproof silence.

'Dukes, how many burned out on the roof?'

'Two.'

'Penhaligon, who survived on the roof? Stop snivelling! Work it out!'

'Nathan. P-perhaps one more.'

'Rumpkin! Who burned out on that roof?

'Ah, Louisa my dear, hello. Definitely your strident, blustering father. Most probably those cheeky little ladies too, which leaves Nathan Glass, the Scion. Yes, the tremors were difficult to decipher with the bloody dragon going off at the same time. This floor is cold. Could you ask housekeeping for a rug, there's a good girl.'

The floor beneath his feet became soft, grey and warm as she walked away. The rats covered the stone in his room completely, clambering and climbing over each other fighting for space. In her distracted state she had not realised he might like this. When she returned to the library Annie reminded her that he liked to kill animals, that it was a mistake and he would enjoy them. Louisa broke down, sat on the library floor and cried. The rats were stuffed and hung like celebration bunting in Rumpkin's room within two days.

The days continued painfully for the Drake children. Routines began to form that would shape their existence. There was one corridor they chose not to walk beyond necessity. There was one room they did not look into if they could avoid it, one person of whom they never spoke. Both Aldemus and Louisa knew that their fury, if released, could dismantle all they were protecting. Yet their desire for revenge against Fifer hung in the air thick like smoke; a volatile hatred held back by the thinnest filaments of gossamer spider silk. Only Aldemus and Louisa's fear of each other's reaction, of setting the other off in that fatal direction, kept them both controlled.

Aldemus's anger drowned in sadness. Louisa's hid behind impassable mountain ranges of practicalities. She kept it there, so it could not reach her, for she was terrified of who she would become if it did.

HERBERT CAVANAGAN

Three Months Later

illicent Savine stood across from Herbert
Cavanagan in the forge.

'I'm not able to. I'm sorry Herbert.'

'But you're the best code breaker, the best!'

She set her work aside. She cleared her head for the
conversation that was about to take place; the same conversation that took place each week. She was stuck in the loop
that ran in Herbert's mind; the circles that he could not free
himself from. She could not free the captives in the castle nor
Herbert; she could just be clear and patient and sit with him
a while.

'This is the greatest work of the magic four. Esther's
Flourishes are in there too: moving constantly, reinforcing
the magic, righting any errors, making it impossible,' she
replied.

'Not impossible! Difficult, but not impossible?'

She looked at his eyes; the whites were painfully reddened, the skin around them set in shades of pencil grey, sunken and dark. His sadness filled the room. She put her hand on his.

'I have tried. It would be difficult from the inside, but it's impossible from the outside. I'm not a match for the magic four. The Scion maybe, but not I.'

'But you'll dedicate your life to freeing your daughter, you won't rest until the magic is lifted, until Fifer is out!'

'I will hope I taught her well.'

Looking lost, he stood and walked around. His face became anguished as his pain intensified.

'This is my fault. If I had not asked for your help, if we had just stayed in Cavanagans like they wanted. I did this! They are dead, because of me.'

She went over to him and placed her hands on his shoulders, held them firmly so that he could not move. She then looked deep into his eyes, which were brimming with tears.

'No. You were curious, like all good magicians. I should never have intervened with that force field. The reason they are dead is because Nathan Glass wanted them dead. The Scion wanted revenge and that is why.'

'My family, my friends, everyone's gone.'

His tears began to trickle down.

'If you need me, I'll be here.'

'No. I'm going home. Just leave me alone.'

He ran out of the forge letting the door slam. She watched as he left, his father's oversized waistcoat flapping around him as he ran away. She rubbed her temples and sat back down. She thought of him for a while and then of Fifer; then she picked up her work and began again.

HERBERT CRIED EVERY DAY. He cleaned and scrubbed Cavanagans; which sparkled and gleamed, bright and proud, but with no Violet and no Fred. There was no one to feel proud of anything he did anymore. And he was a big boy now and a great magician and Cavanagans was his home. He chopped wood every day; all the wood he could find. The trees with agile roots made their way deeper into the forest to avoid the axe. He made piles of wood and built them up like children's towers and totem poles with unhappy faces carved by furious hands. Hands that had grown stronger, that were harder now, calloused and marked from his labours: hands that worked like tools. He carried and chopped and carried and chopped and carved out a way. His softened boyish body became muscular and defined, transformed.

'Welcome to Cavanagans', 'I am Herbert Cavanagan', 'this is my home.'

After the winter ball, at first few people came, then everyone came and there were parcels of cottage pie and looks of sadness and kindness. He did not want this. He wanted his home, no food, no pity, just Cavanagans, like before. Would people just stop crying! He played the piano and everything jarred. He hated their wet faces, too scared to leave, too nervous to return. He chopped more wood. He made a new floor for the terrace that went all the way round the building, then railings, then benches, then a coffin on which he carved his own name.

After neglecting him so cavalierly, fortune seemed to favour Herbert Cavanagan. At his lowest and most self-destructive ebb, two people came unexpectedly into his life, in succession, who would alter the course of it.

The first appeared on the night he thought of destroying Cavanagans, one evening after closing. Everyone had left. The chairs were up on the tables, except the one in which he sat, playing patience. If he won the game he would mop the floor, if he lost, he would burn the building down. The forest was quiet, peaceful, except for the insects' night time songs that he was so familiar with he hardly heard. So when the unkempt pirate forcefully pushed open the door and slammed down a leather case on the table in front of him, sending the cards flying in all directions, any thoughts of potential evening activities were wiped cleanly away. The damp smell of the forest emanated from the pirate's clothes: pine trees, sap and earth.

'Marley Jaker,' said the man in a whiskey gravel drawl, extending his hand, which was sun-worn and nut-brown with dirty fingernails in perfect black crescents.

'Herbert, Cavanagan,' he replied, pleased that he managed to speak.

'I know who you are. I'm a friend of your parents, God rest their souls.'

I know who you are, Herbert thought, but did not say it. The word 'thief!' leapt up in his mind. Marley scanned the room, then moved around with surprising lightness and closed the curtains of every window. He opened up the case. The light and sparkle from within dazzled their eyes. It was bursting with jewellery: gold and silver, diamonds, sapphires, rubies, emeralds, onyx, opal and quartz.

'I've been hiding out with these since the winter ball,'

'I saw you stealing them.'

'Your mother's idea. You were there?'

'For a while. I left before…did you see?'

'No. I left when I had what I needed. I was a risk. With my pockets stuffed, I was a walking bomb. I wish I could have helped them more. I'm so sorry.'

Herbert looked away for a moment, his eyes filling with tears that had arrived unannounced. Marley closed the case and took down a chair to sit on.

'I'm not good on land. I came to the island for the ball and to get me a canine companion. I did not expect to be sleeping in the forest, for months, with a suitcase full of magic explosives. It has taken time, but the ones loaded by Fifer I have neutralised. My attempts to render an amethyst brooch inert have scared all the wildlife from the shoreline of the southern forest and I nearly lost a hand with a gentleman's signet ring, but we're good, they're safe now. I'll be taking those ones back for the sea witches. These are Nathan loaded; I dare not touch, but they are no trouble if left alone in this little case. I'll keep them on my ship. I need to get back to sea. I need to be left alone, for no one to be curious. For that I need you.'

'Why?'

'Because you are a Cavanagan! Your core is good and true, like your parents. These weapons are dark magic, remnants of evil intentions.'

'And bad memories.'

'Yes. They need to leave the island. They will tempt the dissolute, the bored and the crazy.'

'And how do I know you are not one of those?' asked Herbert, surprised at his own daring. Marley's eyes registered shock that turned into amusement.

'You don't. You just have to believe me when I tell you what I want. A simple life, a quiet mind, a peaceful sleep.'

'Yes.'

That was what Herbert also longed for, but feared he would never find. Marley saw the pain on his face and added.

'To let the dark leave for good, a chance for your light to shine.'

It was a bright Saturday, early in the evening and Cavanagans was full. The piano played. A flamenco dancer sat drinking from a tall glass, delightedly showing people her new fan, which opened to the colours of hummingbird wings. People spilled out from the terrace onto the grass. Hawkers and shopkeepers sat in comfortable silence, watching the bees dip in and out of the lavender looking for nectar.

Marley stormed over to Herbert, grabbed him by the waistcoat with both hands and yanked him towards him. Immediately, their faces were uncomfortably close. The face of an angry pirate at such close range was truly terrifying, Herbert acknowledged, before he pushed Marley away. The pirate reeled backwards, though not entirely through force. He gave a loud cry of frustration, then came charging back at Herbert. The hubbub outside Cavanagans quietened; everyone looked in their direction. A crowd gathered. Those who had been at the winter ball had met Marley before. They shuddered as they remembered his face. They felt afraid and believed he was a very bad man, just like Nathan Glass.

'Hit me harder!' Marley hissed, through his expression of fury. Some true anger had risen from his fear of their show not being believed. He added 'or I'll really hurt you.' Then he shoved Herbert back so hard that he fell dramatically to the ground.

People watched intrigued and anxious; all eyes were on them. Herbert did not want to annoy the pirate. He hauled himself to sitting, his heart thumping loudly, as the crowd waited silently. Now was his chance to practise the skills his father had once taught him for defence. He thought about his dad, as he brushed himself down, while Marley taunted him and praised Nathan Glass in front of those watching. Herbert recalled his father's delight in explaining the physics of force. He saw the smile, felt the enthusiasm and remembered the line 'the mighty can fall, if you know how to make them.' He kept that image in his mind: the face of the man he loved and missed with all his heart. Then he stood, his rage flooding through him without being called. He ran forward, got his shoulder in the right position, used his body weight and hoped Marley was ready for him as he made contact.

Marley flew through the air. He landed hard and smacked his head with a loud thump against a tree. Sharp intakes of breath could be heard throughout the crowd. Small flashes like fairy lights appeared before Marley's eyes, moving, like insects crawling and twinkling. 'That's how you do it!' he thought, before it went dark. Herbert stood over him for a few moments. His misty grey eyes flickered, then opened with certainty and Marley jumped up like a hare. He charged dizzily at Herbert and wrestled him to the ground.

'Leave him Marley, he's only a boy!' someone cried.

'He's a Cavanagan!' Marley snarled.

They tumbled and fought, 'Let's use a little fireworks,' said Marley through gritted teeth when their faces were close enough. People were advancing to try and break up the fight. Marley and Herbert parted, panting. Marley extended his arm with a pointed finger and span around on the heel of his worn leather boot. A ring of fire appeared around him and Herbert, giving them space from interference, a circle of tall, golden flames. The crowd stepped a safe distance back. The opaque yellow fire changed to a roaring translucent blue and those who had rushed to climb trees, realised they would have got a better view if they had stayed where they were.

Marching, methodically, line by line, the army came. The ground trembled beneath their synchronised legs moving in time. Advancing from all corners of the forest, they proceed in rows, marching on. Shining, black armour, tilt and down, tilt and down, reflecting the light. From above, the grass was patterned with black warning lines, coming together, blotting out the green.

Surrounding their target the lines responded to every movement Marley made; shift, mirror and move on. They marched through the ring of fire unharmed and waited. The ground was now completely black, except a circle of green by Herbert's feet. The first stag beetle rose and they flew. The air filled with their antlers and black patent bodies. They moved with Herbert's magic, coordinated and connected like schooling fish, to form a tornado shape to engulf Marley. He staggered backwards. The first beetle landed on his face, like an eye-patch, the rest followed in quick succession to surround and submerge him. Marley was floundering beetle-blind in a whirlpool of hard carapaces. Soon his face was covered in a solid mask, he staggered, fell and the crowd screamed. Herbert stood tall.

'Stop! Stop!' shouted Marley, struggling for breath, 'Mercy!'

Dark exoskeletons slammed against his mouth, adhering to it like duct tape. Herbert's nervousness rose up in his stomach. He did not want to speak, but he knew it was up to him to do this, to protect people from Nathan Glass. He rooted his feet into the ground and projected his voice.

'You have disgraced this island. You have chosen to follow Nathan's path of destruction, but you will not pursue it here. I will spare you, but you will leave. Return and I will destroy you. Your ship is ready to set sail. My friends will escort you to your ship.'

Marley nodded his head in surrender. One by one, in single file, like a reel unwinding, the stag beetles flew into the forest.

The crowd had been transfixed. They had not heard the light feet running towards them through the forest. They had not noticed the grey shapes stealthily climbing the trees. Even the teenagers in the trees were not aware of the two monstrous looking beasts that had jumped up quietly to sit behind them, waiting.

When Marley could open his eyes, he shuddered. He was surrounded by the yellow glare of wolf-eyes all focused directly on him. At that moment they jumped down, charged forward, through the flames and arrived at his feet. The crowd screamed and danced around in panic. The wolves circled Marley, snapping their jaws and gnashing their teeth, ferocious in their hunger. One was smaller than the rest, with a very waggy tail, unable to contain his excitement and Marley immediately regretted including him.

Herbert stepped forward to block the view of the youngest wolf. When Marley's feet were free he ran as fast as he could and the wolves gave chase into the forest.

By the time Marley and his companions reached the ship, the wolves' canine teeth had reduced to anatomical correctness; their light, bright eyes had lost the fearsome acid yellow tint: their magical stage make up was gone. The wolves that had remained on board to guard the case now barked in frenzied excitement. Marley threw them all dried beefsteak from his jacket pockets. It was devoured in seconds. Then he was licked and jumped on and loved by his savage pursuers with such wild abandon that he was taken off his feet again. His wolf pack played in the sea and the grime that had made them look more ragged and barbarous came away from their glossy coats. They shook themselves dry.

'Who needs a wash with so many friends to love you?' Marley said. He took off his boots, stepped out of his black trousers to reveal red checked shorts, climbed barefoot onto the rocks then dived into the sea. The wolves picked up driftwood gifts, swam out to the ship, padded onto the deck and made themselves comfortable, while Marley climbed aboard, checked that the case was still safely stored in the hold and prepared to set sail. Marley was glad to be free as the ship pulled away. The wolves howled with louder beauty than in rehearsal, the little one's lungs inflated like the ship's sail and everyone knew the pirate had gone.

. . .

'THE CROWD LOVE it when you use creatures. It will stick in their memory, give them a story to tell and make sure they never forget,' Marley had said to Herbert on the evening that they first met.

'Tigers?' Herbert replied.

'Stay out of the jungle, amplify what you can find in the forest and we'll bring my boys on last,' said Marley.

'Frenzied squirrels? Bad blackbirds?' Herbert said with bitter sarcasm. Marley smiled.

'Oh, I wouldn't mock you. A good magician could make this here playing card terrifying, if he put his mind to it. Let's see what you can do.'

THE GUARDS

*I*n the castle Louisa got up before the others, even before Salem, who had come to rely on her swift, purposeful footsteps past his door and their echo down the corridor as his alarm call. The castle was silent otherwise, the floors cold. She checked the locks of Rumpkin, Savine and Dukes first. Their clever minds were always working to escape, to jiggle a crack in the magic here, prise open something there and confirm that all neural pathways to freedom were indeed still blocked. They were ever watchful for weakness or change, alert for opportunity, to make space for their magic to rise. To do this they had to go through hundreds of ineffective spells each day, thousands if they were particularly motivated, hoping that one would catch.

The Drake children's magic was built on the foundations laid by the magic four. Alone their work might not have been enough to keep the prisoners contained. The captives hoped for inconsistency, weakness, and loose ends; they were disappointed daily. Louisa and Aldemus seamlessly finished what their parents had started and their grip never slackened, captivity was meticulously maintained.

Around her neck Louisa wore a fine gold chain with a spherical crystal pendant. The pendant was set in an ornate golden calyx and it looked like a peony bud about to bloom. Created by Cecelia Riviera and later given to Horatio it was a spy globe, from which any room of the castle could be viewed at anytime. She watched them all, especially the dangerous ones. She observed their behaviour, the different rituals that each performed when they were trying to break the magic.

Fifer Savine often worked into the night and slept through the day, but kept no consistent routine. Nicholas Rumpkin started early, was regimented, performing the same gestures and she assumed the same attempts to break the magic, in the same order each day like an exercise routine. Lady Dukes seemed more prone to agitation and would throw things or herself to the floor in fury then lie in languid despair for hours. She saw their exhaustion and exasperation. She knew how they felt. Hope dies last; a glimmer was all they needed.

She checked the security of their magic each morning and throughout the day and at night if she could not sleep. Sometimes the villains made breakthroughs in understanding the magic, through their constant efforts to destroy it using their minds, devoid of magic power. They could move and nudge things, with concentration to examine how the magic was put together. She could not prevent this. She would have to kill them to do so. They would taunt her with their discoveries. These occurrences were rare and never amounted to any change. Powerless was powerless, but any sign that they had come close to identifying something significant frightened Louisa. She became more vigilant and attended to her routines with renewed, yet nervous energy.

After checking the prisoners she would knock angrily on Aldemus's door, take a deep breath and fling open the curtains. He would rise and together they would secure the rest of the castle before breakfast, which Salem would prepare and Annie may or may not join them for. Sometimes she stayed in bed for days.

The relentless repetition of each day did not soothe Louisa. It kept her on high alert all day and all night, every day and every night. What was that sound? Who's escaped? What's he forgotten? Where's Annie? What was that sound? Check the doors on the second floor. What was that sound?

Once a moth flickered in her peripheral vision and scared her that someone had broken out. She shouted at it; the moth withered and died, fell to her shoulder, its grey-gold wings powder on her black sleeve. When sleep came for Louisa it was light, like mist; if it ever it reached deeper opacity, she would be hurtled from darkness to light and wake in terror.

One morning Aldemus would not rise. He had a cold, he was snoring and his room smelled of sickness. He gestured and grunted clearly his intentions for her to leave, that he would not get up. She said nothing. To secure, check and recheck the castle at the intervals in which they always worked together took her all of the day. Aldemus's methods were different to hers; she learned them and applied them. They were effective although occasionally laborious to perform. She was so exhausted and frustrated when she allowed herself to stop; her stomach so knotted and the thought of food so unappealing that she just lay on the floor of the library. She gazed vacantly at the criss-cross pattern on the ceiling, which looked like white icing on a beautiful cake, a cake she did not want to eat.

Later that day Annie played music in Aldemus's room to cheer him. Louisa recognised songs from her childhood and it felt like recalling a dream from long ago. The music did not move her, as it once would have done. For the next two mornings Aldemus refused to rise. She worked through the day and the night to streamline his methods. She saved ten minutes here, twenty there, but it was not enough, not enough. She could not do this on her own; she could not do this without him.

When he rose four days later, everything was secured and solid except for inside her head, which was light and spinning. She continued door by door, room by room, forcing herself to focus. Every few minutes her concentration fluttered like a bird escaping, without permission. She was relieved Aldemus was up again, but so disassociated from her tense and tired body that anger was numbed and redundant. The path to follow was a well worn track that she steered in mind and body with total absorption. She never rested and all was well, just as the magic four had wished, no one could arrive and no one could leave, but Louisa's mind was slowly unravelling.

In her light-headed wonderings she realised the significance of knowing neither she nor Aldemus could continue this magic work alone. Dependency had always felt stifling; the need for his constant cooperation was as stifling as a sealed stone castle and a thousand repetitive tasks. Annie played melancholy songs on the piano, abstract beautiful music that filled the castle and replaced the silence, but Louisa could not feel them anymore, only register the change when they stopped and the silence began again, when all she could hear was the rhythm of her shoes on the cold stone floors and the echoes bouncing back and around as she walked.

THE EAGLE

*I*n the darkness Esther spent most of her time in
her room.

Nathan was happy or in chronic pain. His left side was
now disfigured, his walk and frame slightly off balance. He
constantly battled with Violet and Horatio's curses, although
they were dead. That morning Violet's name appeared, in her
handwriting, angry weeping scratches along the length of his
arms. The right arm was worse than the left, as Cavanagan
had more letters and cut deeper into his inner elbow. Each
time he moved his elbow joint he opened the wound up.
Healing potions gave temporary reprieve. Each time Betty
bandaged him up, within seconds the name would appear
clear and crisp in red across the white, as if written with a
fine ink pen. But he was happy to be near Esther.

After the turmoil of the winter ball the figments breathed
a sigh of relief. The Firebrand now had a magnificent collar
with brass studs and matching lead, that it had chosen itself.
It was happy to be back, for Nathan to be back. They sat in
the flame room, tense, annoyed with each other, but ulti-

mately comforted by the other's concern. Both silently hoped that the other had learned a lesson. Neither of them wanted to leave the darkness ever again. The thought of it crushed their insides. Nathan created a cool landscape for it to enjoy. The Firebrand was happiest at the top of a snow-capped glacier, on which it could comfortably sit, or on the log flume, especially when Nathan joined it for a ride, but that was not very often. Nathan visited the Firebrand less and less.

No one entered the darkness after Esther, although the miscreants queued and waited and sulked and left. The queues were long. They liked the dance floor. Nathan just wanted to be with Esther. But there was no dancing, no dancing anymore. She did not want to be seen. He understood, he complied, he missed the dancing, but who needed dancing, when you have love? Love conquers all.

The figments had fallen back into a comfortable pattern. Katy was authoritarian and cutting and they all smiled inside. Betty made their tea to the exact requirements of their exacting and pedantic demands. It had never tasted better. The artist painted and the other figments went about their tasks. Everyone was back on cue. Well, nearly, except the Firebrand, who growled each time Esther left her room. They all hated that sound. Jealous they said, protective they soothed, it was still recovering, still getting back to normal. But that noise, that reverberating sound. Make it stop. Betty, tea please. That's better. With each growl something shifted inside. Nathan was busy and busy and in love and the physical pain was sharper than the doubt that grew with each snarl. Paper cut, paper cut, it is nothing really.

And they all played their part and enjoyed their roles and did their best and were exactly who and how they should be. Exactly. Exactly! Something was screaming in the mind of the artist that all was not well. He sensed danger and it felt like icy fingers running up his back. He, as the only one able to hear and confront the truth, walked up to Katy Cavelle and hissed an insult to provoke her. She responded exactly as Katy Cavelle should, but somehow more Katy than Katy ever was.

'Caricature!' shouted the voice in his head.

'You're a caricature!' he yelled at her in exasperation. 'Not yourself!'

She stood very still, looking at him in horror. She wanted to stuff the words back in his mouth so that they could not be true. The screeches of feedback, high pitched and shrill, rang out from the loud speakers. How their heads hurt.

Esther came out of her room. Nathan came out of the contemplation room. The Firebrand roared. The figments ran from all corners of the darkness towards Esther and stood between her and Nathan. She crossed her arms in irritation. Nathan froze. He had heard the dragon, he had seen the figments' reaction and he finally felt the terror in his own heart. He ran back to the contemplation room. Esther tried to run to him, but the figments would not let her past. The contemplation room door slammed shut. The figments all stepped back from Esther, except the artist.

'No love, it's just illusion! There is no love coming from you here in this darkness. Like us, it's all just an illusion! But we see you. The game is up,' he said furiously.

She said nothing and held his gaze with equal intensity. Anger flashed across her grey-blue eyes.

Screeches of feedback rang out again from the speakers, accompanied by the Firebrand's low roar. The cacophony pounded in Nathan's head. He could feel his pulse racing, his heart thudding. He sat on a rocky precipice and covered his ears. In the valley below he watched the water flowing out to the sea in the far distance. He followed its path, watched where it dipped, meandered and looked at the pattern of the currents as they moved along.

He closed his eyes briefly and visualised the essence of himself; the blood in his veins, the life within him, he saw it as pure water streaked with black, a darkness that was closing off the clear channels and would consume him, his arteries tributaries to a black sea. He let the illusion of fresh air caress his face and calm him. His eye caught on a brightly coloured feather that was floating along, bobbing and rising, sinking for a moment, then returning to the rhythm of the river that carried it along. He focused on it, watched it travel. Each time he thought it had sunk for good, it popped back up a little further along, wetter, darker, moving faster, still with colour, so small and far away.

The figments waited, for the calm that accompanied Nathan in the contemplation room. Their breathing became regular once more and their anxiety fell away like autumn leaves. Most returned peacefully to their rooms. A few lingered between Esther and the door. She waited.

The contemplation room door reopened. Nathan re-emerged, closed the door behind him and stood in front of it. His fear was gone. The figments began to drift away. Katy and Betty looked at him at exactly the same moment and at the same time, said gently, so that Esther could not hear,

'Kill her.'

He put his finger to his lips to silence them. They went away. It was just Esther and Nathan and the bass pounding from the empty dance floor somewhere in the darkness. They stood looking at each other waiting. Eventually she spoke,

'I chose cruelty over kindness and that surprises you. It shouldn't. It is challenge, not adoration that I have always wanted,' she said, more sharply than she intended.

'And to feel that you are never good enough, your whole life?' Nathan replied calmly.

'To feel alive, to strive and to dream. To accept the impossible only as the next opponent to beat! Rather than to die of boredom in the world of the most likely.'

'You're romanticising your foolishness. You ran down a well trodden path. Your choice led to what you were trying to avoid, predictability. Predictable old Esther, unoriginal in her miserable marriage.'

'Not always unhappy.'

'Always unloved.'

'Until they came.'

Nathan stared without immediate comprehension.

'My children, that you have mercilessly imprisoned. '

'That you have imprisoned. Your magic, secured by your serpents, what did Violet used to call your Flourishes? The wonderful weavers.'

'You remember everything.'

'Everything.'

'You are the Scion. Set them free.'

'Your Flourishes, your serpents righting any errors any slips that occurred, when you lost concentration, because you did lose concentration, when you were trying to kill me, didn't you Esther? Because they appeared in the courtyard, as you were sealing their fate. If it wasn't for the wonderful weavers then the code breakers inside the castle might stand a chance.'

'Stop! Stop! You did this! Set them free, Nathan, set them free.'

'I don't know if I can.'

A look of horror crossed Esther's face and she stared open mouthed in disbelief, the pretty features of her face distorted to something far from aesthetic perfection.

'Try!' she screamed and lunged forward as if to grab him,

but then slumped to the floor crying and pounding her fists against it. Nathan stood motionless, watched each tear chart its way down the contours of her face, the beautiful face that he had held in his heart for so many years. The heart that had changed so much except for the white speck that stayed constant; goodness ignited by love or wickedness manoeuvring him with illusions of it? It mattered not. All love, all illusion faded fast as he watched her now.

'It would be the last thing I ever did,' he said.

She looked up at him in desperation.

'Please.'

'I loved you once,' he said.

Their eyes locked and her hope evaporated like a fine transparent vapour. The hardness was now visible in his burning amber eyes. Deep in the dark centres she sensed the blackness beyond. There would be no mercy. Esther crumpled to the floor.

Suddenly, the right side of Nathan's body filled with hot searing pain. Simultaneously the left side prickled with icy paralysis. The shackles of Violet and Horatio's curses had awakened and began to fight him, the nerves of his right side jangling in sharp torment, the rest of him leaden and aching. He winced and softly whispered magic to reduce his agony.

Esther lay spluttering and coughing on the ground, choking on her own tears. Her emotions crowded over each other to fill the space where hope once was, despair trampled by anger, clawed back by spite, the whole of her being shook, wanting to hurt him. She stood up, her grey eyes metallic with fire.

'The sphere was mine. The proposal from me,' he said.

'What are you talking about?' she said sharply.

Seconds later he saw the shock on her face as it arrived; as she realised what he meant, as she felt the blow he had just delivered. It winded her and took away both her breath and anger. She felt it in her stomach, as if he had actually punched her, a feeling of sickness that filled her like poison.

'The paintings that hang in Annie's room, that you painted. I came back to the castle once, before the ball, I saw them. Then I knew, for certain, what he had done. You depicted the landscape of my childhood beautifully. It begins at the coppice gate in the snow, which we climb over, then we walk through the meadow, a dry stone wall is on the right, as we head towards the trees. In the distance, hardly perceptible, is the farm where I grew up, a flint cottage visible. The dream ends at the lake, by the cedar trees, in the most perfect spot. The place I loved the most. Love makes fools of us all.'

'Your foolishness Nathan was arrogance and self pity. You were always so needy. I could never have loved someone so unworthy, so ridiculous.'

'Your husband is dead. Your children are imprisoned and you want to taunt me. Go ahead, do your worst Esther, burn out. Die in vengeance mocking my heartbreak.'

'If I cannot burn out to save them, what else is there? But to be the thorn in your side, jagged-sharp and immoveable.'

He looked at her and through her, unmoved. Her fury increased. 'I'm leaving!' she cried. He did not try to stop her as she walked away, as the figments shouted and blocked her path, as the Firebrand roared. Softly he silenced them all so that the only sound was Esther leaving: her angry steps, doors swinging unrestrained and closing in the wind of her departure. He went into the contemplation room. He sat on a rock and looked down at the water. No tears came. In silence Betty called to him, Katy Cavelle hammered on the door and the Firebrand pined, straining at its leash. Nathan felt his heart stretch and hurt in his chest, closed his eyes and listened to it beating, his blood treacle black pumping to oust the light. He surrendered to the darkness inside. His left side now in excruciating pain, the nerves danced with electric current as Violet's curse gained strength. His leg bones began to weaken, perhaps to break as Horatio's curse picked up pace. Too weary to counter their magic he waited for Esther's final blow.

ESTHER STOOD at the edge of the darkness, her eyes momentarily blinded by the daylight from the world she had left behind. The season had changed; there was birdsong, a lark, the aroma of honeysuckle: springtime. Its brightness and joy sent revulsion shooting through her and she doubled over. She saw their faces in her mind, Aldemus, Louisa and Annabelle. Tears streaming, her heart pounding, she clenched her fists to still her shaking body. In her last act there would be no mistake; she was determined and she carefully composed herself. The wild whirling emotions inside her were stilled; she was calm and focused. She stood statuesque and raised her hands above her head, lifted up onto her toes and dived down from the sky with certainty. As she launched herself a razor sharp jab to his side made Nathan flinch. Esther was free falling. She turned into an eagle in her last moments before burning out. No one saw the bird as it plummeted down, nor heard the crash as it hit the transparent magic sealing the courtyard. Esther was gone and her final magic was about to begin.

NATHAN, the Scion, sat alone, all rival contenders eliminated. It was a victory that had wrenched his spine, torn his muscles and left him exhausted from the infinitesimal spells needed to assuage the hate of others. He felt the pain, which let him know he was alive. All he wanted, all he could think as the physical feeling flooded his mind, was that he must speak to Frederick Cavanagan, give him the answers on black hearts and tell him how it actually felt inside. Then he remembered that this could never happen. He experienced this thought without emotion of any kind as the rivers inside him ran dark and deep.

THE EAGLE'S PREY

The eagle's wings were splayed and the feathers flattened. The bright yellow eyes, beady and wide open in death looked down on the courtyard. Nicholas Rumpkin glanced out of his window and looked up at it, longing to possess it. His heart filled with a desire for taxidermy, which momentarily replaced his longing for freedom. Penhaligon, who obsessed over patterns in nature, lamented its fate and began to count its feathers, from the creamy underbelly to the wings and bars of the tail threaded with dark brown. Salem sighed, as he knew he would not be able to clean this roof.

Three days later he stood in the courtyard with Annie and Aldemus looking up at it. The bird's intense eyes seemed to watch the courtyard. With its wingspan outstretched, it looked as if it was waiting to swoop and it cast a sinister shadow.

'I just cannot bear it!' said Annie, 'Our view of freedom obscured by death.' Aldemus gave her a brotherly hug.

'I shall put up a canopy, then you will not be able to see it,' he said.

'But I'll still know it's there, looking down.'

'The more you see it the less it will upset you,' said Salem, 'I've been out here many times and it upset me at first, but now I am used to it. Peculiar as it is I am growing accustomed to this, this circaetinae chandelier hanging above us,' he said with a smile, 'there is beauty in nature, even in death.'

'Not a bird that will wither and decay!' said Annie.

'Circaetinae chandelier,' Aldemus replied, 'Does that mean eagle?'

'Circaetus Gallicus, to be precise. And yes that does mean eagle. Snake eagle.'

'Has Louisa seen it?' Annie asked.

'No. She's not been out for air. She is reading the whole library all over again. Looking for a way out,' Salem replied.

LOUISA'S pale skin contrasted starkly against the rows of mahogany shelves filled with dark green books. She looked up, rubbing her face.

'A dead bird. It shows that the magic on the castle is working. No way in and no way out,' she said.

'Its beak moves when Fifer Savine looks at it,' said Salem.

Aldemus went rigid. Annie looked afraid.

'What do you mean moves?' asked Louisa.

'It's almost imperceptible, but the beak moves when Fifer moves to her window. As if it's grinding its jaw. Penhaligon noticed it. He mouthed to her across the courtyard "It's here for you, Fifer," she and I are good lip readers. She knows.'

Louisa let out a loud sign of frustration and slammed her fist on the desk.

'They shouldn't communicate. More to be done! The high risk ones are closer to the centre and now they're talking!'

'Relax. They have no power,' said Aldemus, leaning against the doorframe.

'No! Aldemus, you sort it out. I can't do everything.'

'Come and see the eagle,' said Salem.

Louisa walked to the nearest courtyard window with them and they looked out at the sharp-eyed bird.

'It's moving its beak now,' said Louisa, 'Fifer must be at the window. Aldemus, turn the windows into mirrors or something. Find a solution. You can do that without going near her. I want to get back to my work.'

'Fifer is fast asleep. Or she was,' said Salem.

'Check,' said Aldemus.

Louisa spun the globe she kept on her wrist and said 'Fifer Savine'. The image of Fifer in her room asleep, curled up on the floor appeared.

'Then which other prisoner is at the window?' asked Aldemus.

'I am,' said Louisa.

They stood in heavy silence contemplating that sad truth. They all knew they were prisoners, but no one, until then, had said it aloud.

Then, unexpectedly, the sound of percussion, of powerful hands tapping out a beat on a wooden table elsewhere in the castle, took their attention. The drumming alarmed everyone, except Annie. She gave a weak smile, which Louisa immediately extinguished with an expression of scorn. Earlier Annie had asked if they could let music permeate the soundproofing. Aldemus had shrugged, while Louisa had given a decisive no. Annie had clearly taken no notice of Louisa. Aldemus looked at them both and shrugged again.

To accompany the beat a mandolin struck up. They heard the sounds of people clapping and slapping their thighs. The musicians sang a bluegrass song about loving chains. Louisa and Aldemus walked away in long, quick strides; Salem followed them. Annie sat on the floor, with her back against the wall for a moment, listening and tapping her feet.

. . .

LOUISA AND ALDEMUS stepped into the courtyard and Salem quickly followed. The temperature dropped. Salem felt the hair prick up from his ears, down his neck and a shiver ran to the bottom of his spine. Chilling air, no breeze. He and Aldemus stood still, watched and waited. Louisa looked upwards, forehead creased as she slowly circled the ground beneath the eagle. A moment later, Annie burst through the door out of breath and it banged shut behind her. Her smile retreated as soon as it had arrived. Every sound she created felt unbearably loud, in the airless silence. She saw their faces, ran to Aldemus and clutched onto him. He held her without taking his gaze from the eagle. The beak opened and closed and repeated its movement, grinding and slow. Louisa surveyed it from all angles. Then, like a match being struck, the wind picked up. Louisa's dark hair flew across her face as she walked. Annie drew closer to Aldemus. The prisoners watched at their windows; Penhaligon, with a restless gaze and nervous eyes, Rumpkin, licking his lips and salivating with lurid eagerness. Lady Dukes was pouting stoically and Fifer's window was empty. Louisa turned to Salem,

'Wake the petite evil, get her by the window.'

Salem left. Soon Fifer appeared yawning and stretching. She took a while to realise that other prisoners were watching her and that all the Drakes were in the courtyard. She stood up straighter. She watched Salem return. Louisa muttered to him, he looked directly at Fifer then directed her to look at the eagle. The wind blew, creating soft shrill sounds as it agitated the air. Fifer looked in the direction in which he pointed. Everyone stood still. She and Louisa looked into the eagle's bright yellow eyes.

The eagle's eyes closed. There was a snap and a crack, as the eagle's broken neck righted itself. The eyes reopened. Its wingspan retracted then outstretched to the furthest point. The eagle rose. The wind punctured the silence, its pitch rising in unexpected crescendos. Annie buried her face in Aldemus's jacket, breathing in the familiar scent. The eagle hovered. Prisoners were coming to the windows to watch.

A bright red undulating line appeared above them. It streaked through the air, beneath the eagle and then vanished. Another, golden yellow, quickly followed. More lines of colour shot across, twisting and writhing. Brief, bright, wavy lines, like scribbles on the invisible ceiling: orange-red, electric blue, bright green. Then slower ones came, slithering; patterns and stripes, hoops and circles of contrasting colour. They raced, a rainbow of bold warning colours, casting shadows on the ground. Snakes.

Salem named every species, softly to himself, to calm his shaking body, until the speed at which new ones appeared made it impossible. Louisa, Aldemus and Fifer's eyes were locked onto every movement. Scarlet, black and yellow ones, banded like beaded necklaces. No one spoke. No one moved. The snakes twisted and threaded, writhed and glided over each other in a chaotic weave, a tapestry of colour above their heads. Their number increased and the light dappled. More and more appeared, the light reduced further and the view of the eagle became obscured. Prisoners were now watching from every window that viewed the courtyard.

Then, the eagle lunged suddenly, downwards in a jerking, jackhammer attack. Snakes rose up, wild movement ensued above. The jabbing beak became visible as holes in the colourful tapestry appeared. With every killing stroke threads disappeared in a flash, snatched and yanked by the eagle's clean, quick, destroying beak. The bird struck again and again charging down fast, furious and focused. As quickly as they had arrived the snakes were all gone. The courtyard was lit by sunshine, under a brilliant blue sky and the watchful vivid eyes of the eagle.

Those eyes seemed to the onlookers to be lit from within, with an incandescent, sun bright, ardent glow. They could not hold her stare and one by one they all looked away. Only when the glare had gone did they dare to look up. The bird had gone. Two bright yellow sapphires sparkling against the blistering blue sky remained. The children immediately recognised the stones.

'Mother!' Aldemus cried, his throat dry. The solid frame that Annie had clung to now quaked in grief. Tears rolled down his cheeks, as Annie sobbed into his wetted lapel. The release of pressure, the tremors, the end of her burn out, felt cataclysmic. Periwinkle Penhaligon bowed his head, out of respect and shame, his tears dropped onto the stone floor. Salem sat in a doorway, slumped and exhausted, his eyes looking up as his body weighed him down. Louisa circled the ground beneath the sapphires, surveying them from all angles; her lips pressed tight, her pallor ghostly. Aldemus joined her beneath the gem stones. In a voice flat and broken he said,

'She's gone. Nathan Glass is the Scion.'

Silent whoops of jubilation, laughter and physical expressions of victory erupted in the rooms behind him, from all the prisoners except Fifer Savine.

'Mother has removed her Flourishes, destroyed them,' said Louisa.

'Her serpents,' said Salem, 'she gave them form.'

'Then there are flaws to be found. You can get us out!' said Aldemus.

'Oh, absolve yourself, Aldemus, why not!'

'Believe me I will try to help! But you could do this, you could work it out.'

'Freedom,' said Salem.

'Or Fifer might,' snapped Louisa.

They all looked for a moment to Fifer who stood thoughtfully at the window, watching attentively. Aldemus could not bear to look at her and turned his back.

'You're better than her,' he said.

'Mother wasn't so sure. Nor am I.'

'I feel sure Esther considers you equal. She wants you free. Fifer might break the code, but she is powerless to act. I believe in you Louisa. A Drake, with a Valencia lineage, what more do you want? You were born for this,' said Salem.

'The magic they created is intertwined, moving around us constantly. How can we ever find a flaw?' asked Aldemus.

'It is in the timing, in understanding the pattern. If a flaw appears, as a way out it will be momentary, lasting seconds or minutes if we are lucky. It will never appear in the same spot and the size of the exit will vary, depending on how the layers part. One might not appear for fifty years,' said Louisa.

And with that, a yellow sapphire fell through the magic above them and landed on the grass next to them. The second stone rolled to where the first had fallen through, but remained above them. Annie gasped, then clasped her hands together. Aldemus picked up the stone and smiled at Louisa.

'Flaws to be found, flaws to be found!' Rumpkin sang out like a market trader, 'one a penny, two a penny, flaws to be found!'

'The race is on ladies, the race is on!' shouted Lady Dukes.

'Let the women tear each other apart!' cried Rumpkin gleefully.

'Go, go go!' shouted Lady Dukes, smiling frighteningly.

'Penhaligon! Penhaligon, what are the odds? Fifer Savine versus Louisa Drake. Let that mathematical mind of yours cavort and cartwheel. I'll bet you all my turkey sandwiches and a stuffed chinchilla on this one!' said Rumpkin.

'We can hear them talking! We shouldn't be able to!'

Louisa snapped at Aldemus angrily, 'Do I have to do everything?' For once, Aldemus did not bite back. He did not let her irritation crush the hope that was fast rekindling inside him. Then suddenly came a wall of sound.

'Freedom!' In full volume the Harleshamp band's music reverberated around the castle. Prisoners who knew the song joined in rattling and banging any objects they could get their hands on. Voices sang out.

Louisa made a fast sweeping arm movement. Down came the mirrored glass, cutting through the air, window by window, slamming shut with weight and force. Mirrors that dropped like guillotines to soundproof the castle. The final window melded with the stone and there was silence. The mirrors faced into the courtyard and reflected Louisa's glare into infinity. Her sharp posture, with arms held aloft and Aldemus's solid stance as he held the crumpled weight of Annie, was multiplied all around them.

THE SCION

$\mathcal{K}$aty had been watching Nathan closely. He slept less and it showed in the grey crescents beneath his eyes. His lean form had reduced, he was almost scrawny and his vitality was missing, unlikely to return soon. Beyond the physical agony, which he was managing more effectively every day, there was a worrying change, a more debilitating one: his fear. It was forceful, unwavering and felt deeply by all of the figments. Some took action by boarding up doors, windows and the entrance to the darkness. Nathan wanted no more visitors. The banging echoed through Katy's tortured mind. His physical weakness could be overcome, but this psychological chasm, maybe not, she thought. She oversaw the work of securing the darkness from the outside world. It lessened the pinch of his anxiety, which howled through her veins and did not abate until the job was done. Afterwards she felt his relief surge through her.

Nathan never wanted to leave the darkness again. He had not said this, but the Figments felt it like burning rocks in their heads. It made the artist swear in Italian and German, from his new repertoire of obscenities. Betty shook her head despairingly and quiet weeping became her pastime. Everything about Katy was now as sharp as fingernails running down a blackboard. The rest adapted in their own beautiful and spiteful ways.

The Figments set to work enhancing the vistas contained within. Cherry blossoms against a bold blue sky for spring, maple trees turning red for autumn, winter walks amidst snow-topped pines and hot summer sun by cool clear sea. They created scents to elevate his senses and divert his thoughts. Of course, none of it was real, but Nathan did not want real. Real was bad, imagination was good.

Katy did not want Nathan to be weak. This thought buzzed incessantly in her head. He was wired differently now, incorrectly, his clarity muddied. Lurking inside her was the feeling of contempt. His own power was aligned against him, like a gun to his head. Nathan saw the barrel of the gun and said a silent thank you that the Scion's magic was unbeatable. Unbeatable, at least for his generation in this moment, it gave him space to breathe, to fall apart.

Nathan sometimes wanted to leave the contemplation room, but when he tried to his heart rate would sound loudly in his ears, like the hooves of a stampeding herd. Then nausea would rise up inside him and close him down. A feeling that advanced and receded like gentle waves upon a shore. He would forget the desire to leave and would lay on the floor to feel something stable, from which he could not fall. The moment of intention was gone floating up, up and away like a helium balloon.

Betty would hear him stumble and come into the room pulling her cardigan around herself. She would place a tweed blanket over him, which she had edged with russet velvet and on which she had carefully embroidered Scion in the corner.

Katy would later find him, look upon his collapsed figure with a clenched expression and eventually help him up. He would sit like a frightened child, with his eyes closed and listen for the click as she closed the door behind her. She could not help him. She felt trapped in an unbreakable cycle. 'Gone' was a place she quietly longed for, to be blown out like a candle in the darkness.

MILLICENT AND ELLA

*A*fter Marley's dramatic intrusion, the second person to alter the course of Herbert's miserable existence was Millicent Savine. She arrived at Cavanagans one evening with three new axe heads for him. Her timing was opportune, although he no longer wanted to chop wood. Marley had gone. The job was done. The melancholy had set in again, heavy as lead. He was waiting for the last guests to leave the forest safely; then he was going to set Cavanagans on fire. Millicent seemed to know. She said nothing, packed him a bag and, with a forthrightness he dared not challenge, she took him to the forge. She would fix him. He would stay with her. She would bring in Ella.

Ella was the tailor's daughter who made and repaired Millicent's clothes and worked in the shop, three doors down. She was about the same age as Herbert and one of the few people the blacksmith talked to. Over the years Ella's bonhomie had slowly chipped away at Millicent's guardedness, despite her best efforts to be purely nonchalant and transactional in conversation. Ella was intrigued by the woman her little brother called the fire-witch. The black-

238

smith-fire-witch had been a tough nut to crack with cheerfulness, although Ella kept trying.

Then, one day in the busy tailor's shop, Millicent was waiting in line watching Ella deal with a sour and unreasonable customer. He was painfully annoying and taking far too long as far as Millicent was concerned. She tapped her foot in irritation as she listened to him whining and getting nasty, when Ella again refused to do what he wanted. Ella clearly and politely said no, for the fourth time. To which he responded with a spiteful, personal insult. Ella's good humour finally vanished. Pink-cheeked and flustered, she replied to his last barbed remark with and daring and witty rebuke. Millicent was shocked; and then delighted by Ella's bravery and laughed extremely loudly. The laughter surprised all three of them. The customer left the shop storm-faced and huffing. Millicent grinned at Ella, admiring her audacity and Ella grinned back happily, knowing her work was done.

Later that day, heartened and happy, Ella set to work making the blacksmith a bandana from offcut fabric, embroidering it with a bright sun in orange and gold thread. She placed it between the folds of a repaired leather apron. When Millicent found it she smiled and thought, for the first time, that the town was not so bad. From then on Ella's family were never short of good hammers or nails and Millicent's collection of headwear expanded gradually over time, becoming edgier and more pleasing.

That was long before the winter ball. Before Millicent found out Fifer was imprisoned, before Millicent's world became grey and pointless. Ella and her family were kind and compassionate to Millicent. She did not know how to respond. When they came to see her she stood awkwardly, as uncomfortable looking as the flowers they had given her, which stood splayed and incongruous in a iron kettle. Their concern bewildered her and almost washed over her, as nothing could make this better. Their concern seemed point-less, until she thought of something practical she could do with it: give it to Herbert.

So Herbert arrived at the forge with a heavy bag that he carried lightly and grief that weighed him down. Ella would come each day with a little soup, a listening ear, a big-hearted smile and sometimes an almond pastry or a cherry slice. Herbert hardly noticed, but the persistence of kindness in gestures small and regular continued. Millicent observed with wonder how Ella seemed to know exactly what he needed: time alone or attention, care or distance, silence or conversation. Effortless it appeared, but Millicent felt she was watching a scientist with carefully prepared, exact measures. When Herbert could eventually lift his head from the abyss of sadness and see Ella, each day grew a tiny bit sweeter or at least not as chokingly bitter.

Ella would appear with walking boots for him on days when the sky was blue and the air was cool. She took him to lakes and rivers in places he had never visited before. On some outings he would not say a word. On too-chilly days she lent him books to distract his troubled mind. He did not always read them, despite Millicent repeatedly placing them in his eye-line. But sometimes he did, sometimes he got lost in them for hours.

Months later, when, eventually, a little colour came in his cheeks, when sleep was not so elusive, Millicent taught him how to really play with fire in the forge. He hammered shapes of abstract form, pounded them almost flat. They were dented, peculiar and battered looking things. 'Like a tray trampled by horses,' Millicent thought to herself, when he first made one. He continued making theses 'peculiarities', as Millicent referred to them when talking to Ella, for some time. Ella mounted them on the back wall like paintings.

Millicent's watched her baffled, but did not object. Then he made a pendant for Ella that was supposed to be a flower, but looked like a beer bottle top. Then he made a wonky pair of scissors, which showed his great progress and looked a bit like a hornbill. These experiments built his confidence to start on the big project. The work that would let him hammer from dusk till dawn, the creation that let him smash away his pain, perfect his craft, and evaporate his loneliness. The red-hot coals were a safe place he could always come in the moments when the world seemed fine to everyone else, but he needed to smack something really, really hard.

Over time he was able to help Millicent, he mastered forging techniques and became useful. He enjoyed the complete absorption that the job required to stay safe and avoid danger. It occupied him and enabled him to maintain a level of calm for long periods of time. In the evenings he worked on the project that was to consume him until its completion, a magnificent archway with wrought-iron gates. Millicent let him continue in the forge when her work was done. He considerately used magic to create perfect silence so he could work into the night and she could sleep peacefully. She gave him complete freedom, but spun a discrete spell, a wildcat alarm to puncture the artificial silence, should his concentration ever wain.

He hammered gates that Dante would have been proud of. His artistic vision was strong and clear. Months passed by and the structure grew larger. Outings with Ella continued and he looked forward to them. She made him black bandanas embroidered with red and gold images: flowers, beetles and patterns that suited him. He wore one everyday to keep his hair from his face and he thought of her each morning when he selected one. The seasons passed by and Herbert remained in the heat with the anvil and hammer, drawing, bending and fastening metal.

When the day came that he finally finished the gates, he took them, as he had always planned, and assembled them at the entrance to the southern forest. He set the tall iron structure at the point where the path to the castle began. With the help of a little magic they stood elegant and imposing. Ella had joined him, knowing what an important moment it was for him, wearing her special flower pendant. She admired his craftsmanship and efforts. He hoped she would be impressed by his use of magic in construction, the perfect angles, the solid foundation, the spirit level accuracy, but she was just happy to see how amazingly well he looked. His smile was pure delight, its existence and the beauty of it, of him in full radiance shining and alive. It was all she needed in this world.

They stood looking up at the iron spikes and spirals, the unfurling leaves and furious circles of beauty. The lines that curved in the centre converged to form the shape of a heart. It was a fierce and passionate shape, devoid of sentimentality, its centre directly level with Herbert's eyes. Ella felt a stab of intense sadness when she realised the heart would split perfectly in half when the gates were opened.

'What do you think?' Herbert asked tentatively.

'They are just so impressive, really beautiful,' Ella said.

Herbert's mood was buoyant and he put his arm around her and squeezed her.

'Aren't they. Thank you. I'm pleased. I'm so glad you're here,' he said and enveloped her in big hug. She hugged him back with all her might.

'So am I. Well done Herb.'

They separated and held hands for a moment, still looking at up the gates.

'They need to be open,' Herbert said.

He unlatched them. They each took one side and set the gates wide open. The air was fresh, the ground slightly damp.

They stood before the archway taking in and commenting on the curlicues set high above them. Ella congratulated him on his spirit level accuracy. They stood holding hands and smiling. Then explosions of pastel colour appeared suddenly in mid air, like paint splashes. The colours interwove and formed a ribbon around the gates that read 'Grand Opening!' and tied in a perfect bow before them. She smiled. He grinned and looked at her in surprise.

'Yes. I'm quite shy about it. Minor magic. Haberdashery mostly. I don't tell many people.'

He hugged her.

'It's wonderful,' he said.

She laughed. She handed him the wonky hornbill scissors that he had made, over a year ago, so that he could cut the ribbon. She clapped and smiled proudly. He bowed graciously and his smile widened. They stayed at the edge of the forest all day matching each other's magic, playing games for their own amusement, until the iron gates were silhouetted against a sunset sky fading to dusk. They wrapped the ribbon like a scarf around their shoulders. Ella went back with him to Cavanagans, where he returned for good that evening, and she never really left.

Ella and Herbert's lives fitted together seamlessly, uplifting them both. Love was warm and tingling, with runaway smiles and and peacefulness. One day Herbert was brave and he asked Ella to be with him forever, and she said yes.

Herbert went back to the forge to tell Millicent and to thank her. His words were heartfelt and emotional as he stood before her, stuttering through burst of tears and smiles. Her reply was gracious and reserved, but her happiness at seeing his happiness was genuine and inescapable. He felt it and she knew. They parted formally, as life-long friends.

They married in the spring beneath the arch of the gates; when the blossom fell like snow confetti and the daffodils were trumpets all around heralding life and joy and new beginnings. Herbert wore violets on his lapel, Ella a dress she had made. Millicent attended in warm colours with a warmer smile. Somewhere on the ocean, in the evening, Marley raised a glass and his good wishes up to the night sky, full of stars. In Cavanagans the dusty piano keys played until the early hours and something felt better inside.

EPILOGUE

$\mathscr{L}$ ove can set castles ablaze and send storms into the coldest winters. Heartbreak bleeds black for magic minds. Nathan's heart is getting darker and his may not be the only one. Louisa, Annie, Aldemus, Fifer, Herbert and Ella all await their fate in book two, The Prison.

Darkness and Light Series

If you wish to find out about the next book release please
visit JMHendrikx.com
The Castle is the first book in the Darkness and Light series.
If you enjoyed this book, please consider leaving a review
online, even if it's only a line or two, it will be greatly
appreciated.

Acknowledgements

MY HEART CHEERS loudly and somersaults over and over in gratitude to Philip, Susannah, Cat and Daisy whose amazing minds and generous help improved this story. This book is dedicated to Philip and Nikita who encouraged me to walk bravely on to the page. And to my children, the brightest lights in my universe. Thanks also to my friends and family for all of your support. I am forever grateful.

Printed in Great Britain
by Amazon